THE

EATER

OF

DREAMS

THE
EATER
OF
DREAMS

KAT CAMERON

thistledown press

Thistledown Press Ltd.
410 2nd Avenue North
Saskatoon, Saskatchewan, S7K 2C3
www.thistledownpress.com

Library and Archives Canada Cataloguing in Publication
Title: The eater of dreams / Kat Cameron
Names: Cameron, Kat 1964- author.
Description: Short stories.
Identifiers: Canadiana (print) 20190137436 | Canadiana (ebook) 20190137444 | ISBN 9781771871846 (softcover) | ISBN 9781771871853 (HTML) | ISBN 9781771871860 (PDF)
Classification: LCC PS8605.A4818 E28 2019 | DDC C813/.6—dc23

Cover and book design by Jackie Forrie
Printed and bound in Canada

Canada

Canada Council
for the Arts

Conseil des Arts
du Canada

SASKATCHEWAN
ARTS BOARD

cultivating
the arts

Thistledown Press gratefully acknowledges the financial assistance of the Canada Council for the Arts, the Saskatchewan Arts Board, and the Government of Canada for its publishing program.

THE
EATER
OF
DREAMS

For my family

CONTENTS

CONTENTS

Spirit Houses

O N NEW YEAR'S DAY, I meet an old friend at the Muttart Conservatory. It's minus twenty-five outside, but inside the air sweetens with perfume from the table of pink and purple hyacinths for sale.

At Maureen's side, her three-year-old daughter, Emily, dances in perpetual motion. Her pink sweater with an appliquéd daisy shimmers with colour, as bright as the hyacinths, and her Hilary Duff jeans have pink and silver sequined butterflies at the cuffs. I feel drab and oversized beside this pint-sized fashion plate.

Maureen has brought another woman with her, Jasmine's mother, whose name I can never remember. While they are hanging up their heavy winter coats, I smile and nod, hoping that Maureen will introduce her name in conversation.

The lobby branches into four corner ramps. Below four glass pyramids are different display areas: temperate, tropical, desert, and a feature show. As we walk up towards the desert pavilion, heavy doors swing open. Emily darts ahead.

"Careful," Maureen calls.

The pavilion glows beneath the bright blue sky. Dry desert air. I inhale deeply and smell sage. Blooming prickly pear with red bumps of fruit fill the middle bed, limbs coiling like octopi.

A massive saguaro stretches up to the glass. Emily reaches out to grab a fistful of cactus.

"Sweetie, that's sharp," Maureen says, pulling back Emily's hand. Emily pouts for a second, reaches out again. Maureen patiently pulls back the tiny hand. I'd let Emily touch it for herself. Once pricked, twice shy. Perhaps Sleeping Beauty was an overindulged child, unafraid of evil witches and spindles.

Jasmine runs along the path ahead of her mother who is encumbered with the stroller, diaper bag, sweater, purse. Jumping up onto the concrete retaining wall, Jasmine begins throwing fistfuls of gravel on the path.

Bending down, I say, "Don't do that. The plants need the gravel to live."

Her mother glares at me. I feel like pointing out the signs. *Stay on the path. Don't pick the flowers.* Why does everyone feel exempt from these rules? The mother is too passive to complain openly; instead, she stuffs Jasmine into the stroller. Jasmine begins a high-pitched whining, like a dentist's drill.

We walk down the ramp and over to the temperate area. The trees are dormant, brown leaves scattered in a creek below. Only the ivy covering the lone stone walls shows a hint of green. I sit on a bench under a bare oak tree, covering my mouth to hide the yawns.

Jasmine's mother turns to Maureen. "Someone was up late partying. Remember those days?" Her tone is mildly patronizing, as if speaking of a teenager rather than a woman her own age sitting right in front of her. "We were in bed last night by nine. We saw the early fireworks and that was it."

I smile, say nothing. I was up late doing lesson plans, but if she wishes to envy me, she can. It's better than the mild contempt I so often feel from mothers my age. When did my life become a joke? I don't know what Maureen has told her about me. Maybe I'm a cautionary tale, the kind told in whispers.

We wander under the bare trees and then back down the ramp, park the strollers by the coffee counter, and buy coffee and date squares. Once the two little girls are settled at a small table, with paper and crayons, Maureen mentions the tsunami that hit Asia on Boxing Day.

"I keep thinking about this one mother." Maureen turns to Jasmine's mom. "Andrea, have you seen her? The Australian mother and her two boys. She couldn't swim with both children and had to choose to hold on to one. Imagine."

"Sophie's choice," I interject. They both stare at me blankly. "Remember, Sophie had to choose one of her children or the concentration camp guard threatened to take both."

"Oh, the movie," Andrea says slowly. "But this is real life."

What does she think the book was based on? Andrea is the type of woman who proudly claims to read only non-fiction. I can't understand why Maureen spends so much time with her.

Maureen returns to the Australian woman from the news. "I don't know how she could make that choice."

"Would it be better if she had left both to die?" I ask. Even though both children lived, thousands of nameless children died, both local and tourists. Do the media focus on this story to take our minds off the other mothers, the ones whose children didn't survive? Discussing this topic makes me feels as if we're trying to ward off disaster. Not here. Not us.

"Remember our trip to Phuket?" I ask Maureen, changing the topic. "The Friendly Garden B&B? Remember the two fat German guys in their fifties who were sharing the Thai prostitute?" Every morning, over tea and toast, we'd see the Germans at the table next to ours, their thick voices rattling like gunshot. Two sunburned beefy faces glowing on either side of that sulky silent teenager.

"I don't remember them," Maureen says. Wilful amnesia. Or maybe pregnancy does destroy brain cells.

"Oh, come on. You were the one who started calling them the Tom Thumb Twins. The prostitute was a head taller than either of them."

"There are children present," Andrea says in a prissy voice. It's lucky I didn't mention the Australian surfboarder Maureen picked up the second day there. I'd gone for a walk, came back to our tiny villa draped with pink bougainvillea, caught Maureen and the tanned beachboy doing it doggy style on the sagging double bed. I backed out the door fast. The secrets I could tell. The secrets she could tell. What old friendship consists of, secrets you could tell but won't, not even when the friendship is dying, pulled apart by too many changes.

I drink my coffee, listening to Maureen and Andrea discuss daycare options. Looking at Maureen, I can see traces of the bohemian backpacker who trekked through Thailand with me. In her twenties, Maureen wore her black hair in a pixie cut that feathered her high cheekbones. Since Emily's birth, she's been growing it out and there are streaks of grey at the temples. With the shoulder-length bob, the black Gap sweater and tan pants, she looks like the mothers she used to mock, .the ones who thought little Ashley was a genius even though she couldn't spell *genius* in grade seven. She has achieved that adult look, that adult life: house, husband, child. One version of an adult life.

The first year of our MA program, Maureen broke up with her boyfriend, a jerk who slept with another woman. The night after Maureen's final crying phone call, we started drinking Cabernet Sauvignon in our apartment, and then hit the local pub when the wine ran out. By two, she was flashing her breasts at the guys in the bar. I dragged her out.

On the way home, a frosty November night, she started screaming at the moon like a madwoman. "Fucking men. Assholes. No more fucking men for me." She wouldn't shut up. I walked her around the downtown area for an hour, afraid to take her home, worried that our neighbours would call the cops. Now she acts like butter wouldn't melt in her mouth. It's all worked out for her.

In Thailand, we saw a woman carving flowers out of vegetables, daikon transformed into white leaves, turnips into tulips. I bought an elaborate red rose, carved from a beet, and placed it ceremoniously on the verandah of the next spirit house we saw, an elaborately carved, miniature teak dwelling, its swooped roof draped with garlands of marigolds. Every Thai house has a spirit house, a *sarn phra phun*, built on the northeast corner of the property to placate the spirits of the land, the *chao tee*, displaced by the building. Rules structure the placement: the shadows from the main house cannot fall on the spirit house or bad luck will follow. Each day the householder places offerings of tea, rice, and flowers at the door of the spirit house to propitiate the gods.

Shut out of the conversation, I finish my coffee and announce, "I'm heading up into the show pavilion."

"Me go too," Emily says.

Maureen looks at me doubtfully.

"Sure, come on," I say, annoyed that Maureen questions my ability to watch her child for ten minutes.

Emily dashes ahead, her shoes clattering on the tiles. The doors swing open to a garish display of red, a womb of poinsettias, with one giant Christmas cracker spilling papiermâché candy over the central bed.

I sit on a bench and watch as Emily runs round and round the central bed, a top spinning out of control. Look at me! Look at me! She takes after her mother. Fortunately, there's no one else in the room with us, and I indulge her until she staggers, dizzy with motion, and plops down hard on the floor.

"Let's look at the flowers," I say, before she can start to cry.

We bend over the mass of potted plants. The poinsettias glow like hard candy. Their colour entices Emily, who reaches for the petals. I remember they're poisonous.

"No, we don't pick the flowers. Leave them for other people to enjoy." That lecturing tone. I'm withering into a pursed-mouth schoolteacher. A caricature. I despise this role, which is forced on me more and more often. In any case, it does no good, for Emily doesn't listen. She grabs, pulling petals.

"Emily, I said no." Reaching over, I attempt to pry open her fingers, extract the treasure. She holds on, clenching chubby fingers tighter around the petals, which ooze like blood. But I'm stronger and I win, forcing her hand open, brushing the petals back onto the black dirt. Fighting down the temptation to give her a sharp smack on the hand, I say, "They're poisonous. Don't pick poinsettias."

Emily throws herself on the tiled floor, stretched full length in a display of grief. "No, no, no." A word she knows well.

"Emily, the floor is dirty. Get up."

She ignores me.

"Fine." I'm not about to reach down, haul her up by the arm, an action I've seen many exasperated parents perform, the grab and yank, the suppressed exclamations to stop crying, act your age. I walk over to the bench, sit down.

Emily continues her prima donna act, fake sobs and all. I wonder if it works at home. Would it work if I were more emotionally attached?

Last year, Emily fell off a slide at the playground and cut her chin.

"When I saw her," Maureen said, after the trip to Emergency, after the tears and comforting, when the only remaining evidence was two tiny stitches, barely visible, "when I saw Emily with blood pouring down her face, I realized that a piece of my heart is outside my body."

A ludicrous statement. I would never have expected Maureen to say something like that. It's as if giving birth has destroyed her sense of humour. Yet I could also understand. The power of a metaphor — your heart outside your body. A piece of you, gone.

Are there spirit houses for lost children, the ones who haunt your house? She was so small, my lost child. Born two months early. I'd been so sure, even after three miscarriages. Sure that everything would work out.

We named her Spirit. The grief counsellor at the hospital told us to pick an unfamiliar name. Ryan wanted something else, but I insisted. I insisted on the picture too, her small form swaddled in blankets, her face blue, like the statues I saw in Bangkok. Every week I place flowers before my makeshift shrine.

I look up and Emily is just disappearing, a blur of pink running down the broad ramp. The hydraulic doors swing wheezily closed and she's gone. Jumping up, I run after her.

Maureen and Andrea are at the table. Jasmine sits placidly in her stroller, clutching her panda with the ripped ear.

"Where's Emily?" I ask. "Did she run down here?"

"She's missing?" Maureen jumps up, grabbing her black sweater at her throat. The gesture is so histrionic that I want to laugh. But don't.

"Where is she? Why did you let her out of your sight?"

"I told her not to pick the flowers and she took off. The doors open automatically."

Maureen is already gone, running towards the entrance. I hear her crying breathlessly, "Did a little girl in a pink sweater run by?" but I don't hear the reply. I walk up the ramp to the Temperate Pavilion, calling "Emily." I won't run in a gesture of panic. Unless she managed to open the double glass doors leading outside, she's still in the building, probably hiding in one of the other pavilions. I often play hide-and-seek at her house, counting to ten while she hides behind bathroom doors and under beds. "Where's Emily," I'll call before she pops out of her hiding place, screaming, "Here I am." For her, this is a game.

I try to believe this. There's no sign of her as the doors swing open. Images flash through my mind: Emily hit by a car in the parking lot, Emily kidnapped, Emily face down in the pool of water below the bare elm trees. All it takes is one instant of inattention. All my fault. Like the wicked fairy at the christening, I trail bad luck behind me.

"Emily," I yell. No answer. She's hiding. I know she's hiding. But my heart pounds in my ears so that I can barely hear. I can't catch my breath. "Emily."

Beneath a bare magnolia tree, an elderly couple sits on a bench. Both white-haired, shrunk into themselves.

"Is Emily about this high?" the man asks, holding the flat of his palm at the level of the bench's back. I nod. "She ran up that way."

I hurry around the curving path, past the goldfish pond, the oak trees with a few clinging dead leaves, the rhododendron bushes. At the little bridge, Emily leans over the top log, staring down into the water.

"Emily, why did you run away?" I grab her arm as she attempts to sprint by me. She pulls. I swing her up on my hip. "You scared me." She hides her face in my shoulder. "I'm sorry," she whispers. How quickly we learn that word and its power. I hug her, feeling that fragile vulnerability of small limbs.

I walk slowly down the ramp. "She's here," I call at the bottom. "She's fine."

Maureen rushes over and grabs Emily from my arms. A sudden emptiness. I'm reminded once again of my insignificance to their lives. I should feel relief. Instead, thick anger surges through me, so strong I cannot speak.

I walk away. Maureen calls my name, but I ignore her. Pulling on my coat, I push open the outside door, which would have been too heavy for a small child to open. I know Maureen believes that somehow I broke the rules, didn't placate the spirits, left some rite undone. She has backed away, afraid that my bad-luck shadow will fall upon her house.

Whyte Noise

COMING OUT OF A BAD relationship, Zoe retreated to Edmonton. Late July she found a place in the Strathcona district. A tiny apartment, it was up three flights of purple stairs with a bedroom under eaves so low she couldn't stand up in the corners, a short hallway, and a kitchen/living room with large windows looking out into the branches of an elm tree. She liked the idea of living in a garret. There was a decayed charm in the sloping chipped walls, in the canopy of green elms lining the streets, in the university area with its coffee shops and bars.

The house sat on a corner lot. Built as a single-family home in 1918, it had slipped down the social rung into a boarding house for unwed mothers in the twenties, bottomed out as a rooming house in the dirty thirties. Converted to a hospice for parents with terminally ill children, it had recently been bought by an older woman with crinkly grey hair.

The first month Zoe melted. August heat collected under the eaves, pooled in the low corners. During the evening, she sat in a lawn chair on the fire escape, drinking strawberry daiquiris in blue-stemmed glasses with her new boyfriend. The sun set in orange strips behind the cardboard skyline. At night she left the windows open. Her boyfriend, Grant, radiated like a furnace. They kicked off the blanket and sheets and set a small rotating fan on the floor with a bucket of ice in front of it. The fan oscillated slowly, each pass of cool air soothing her prickly skin. One night she straddled Grant, rubbed ice cubes over his chest, goose bumps flaring under her fingertips.

Each weekend as the bars on Whyte Avenue closed, crowds of students would stumble by, boisterously shouting "Fuckin' A, man!" and other profanities punctuated by "Whooo-hoo" catcalls. A drunken nocturnal parade. One night a girl screamed. Primal screams. No words, just the sound of a jet engine taking off. A scream queen in a B-grade flick. They looked outside. A girl in a short green coat, a man in a leather bomber jacket. Standing five feet apart, they faced each other, a showdown without guns. The woman screamed again.

Grant pulled on his jeans and went downstairs. Hiding behind the bedroom curtains, Zoe stared out into the dark streets, envisioning a fight, a knife. But the couple maintained the distance between them. Grant hovered around the edge of the bubble they created. Zoe couldn't hear what he said. The woman stopped screaming, started walking away.

Grant came back upstairs. "She said she was okay. I don't think there's anything else I can do. She didn't want me to call the police."

Now that the noise had stopped, Zoe was shaking.

"Hey, it's okay." He pulled her into a bear hug.

She knew she was safe with him.

It took three weeks to get her cable connected. The repairman finally showed up, tested the line, banged around in the basement, and ran some new wires. He told her to contact her landlady. When Zoe phoned, the landlady said reproachfully, "I can't afford all these repairs. The previous tenant never complained." No surprise there. The previous tenant, a six-foot man, had lived simply: a futon on the floor, one wooden chair with broken slats propping up a battered acoustic guitar, a sprawling stereo system, and a jungle of pot plants in the living room. Zoe had scrubbed the tile floors for two days, removing rings of grime left by months of mouldy plants, restoring the floor's terracotta shade.

Each morning at seven, the derelict squatting downstairs woke up. He'd stumble onto the balcony directly below her bedroom window. Five minutes of hacking followed, the deep coughing of an emphysemic patient. Then he'd spit several times into the garden below and light the first cigarette of the day, the acrid smoke drifting into her bedroom. She'd get up, slam the window shut, and then crawl back into bed, pulling a pillow over her head.

One day she passed him on the second-floor landing. He stank of stale beer and American cigarettes. Unshaved, unkempt, he was dressed in baggy grey track pants and a loose T-shirt with some long-forgotten band on the front, probably bought for three dollars at Value Village. She averted her eyes, feeling angry at his intrusion into her space. Angry that he made her feel guilty. The second-floor apartment was rented by a girl with platinum hair streaked cotton-candy pink; most days she wore purple striped leggings under an oversized wool coat.

She'd bang out of her apartment at eight each morning, thud down the stairs, and slam the door like a petulant teenager.

After a month of this routine, Zoe phoned to give notice.

"I know, I know," the landlady apologized. "I've been trying to get him evicted all month. He was kicked out of his apartment so he's staying with his daughter. He's a bottle picker and an alcoholic. I've had complaints, let me tell you."

He was gone the next week, but the front door, its lock jammed, still swung open to every intruder.

In October, the landlady refused to turn on the electric heating. "Here," she said, lugging in two filthy oil heaters, "you can use these. Last year, this apartment cost $100 a month to heat and I can't afford that." As the temperature dropped below zero at night, Zoe's breath fogged the air while she watched late-night TV, huddling under three comforters. Her right elbow ached in the cold.

She hurried down the narrow staircase one morning, late for class. Her ex was standing in the hallway. She stumbled, catching at the banister.

"What the hell are you doing here?"

"Hey, it's good to see you too." He loomed over her, his arm barring the exit. She retreated up two steps.

"How did you find out where I live?"

"A woman at the university gave me your address." He could be very charming. She had an unlisted phone number. She'd had a restraining order against him in Vancouver. He had maxed out their credit card and when she wouldn't give him more money, when she kicked him out, when she changed the locks, he started showing up at the Shopper's where she worked. One night he followed her home, five paces behind her, swearing under his breath. "Bitch. Cunt. Whore."

"I think you should go." She clipped her consonants like bullets firing. When he didn't move, she backed up slowly until she reached her apartment and clicked the deadbolt shut.

That night she couldn't sleep. She wedged a chair under the broken lock of the back door and sat at her kitchen window, staring out at the tattered yellow leaves still attached to the elm. Around her the apartment creaked and groaned, the ghosts of past alcoholics, unwed mothers, parents with dying children, all emitting pain like a buzz saw in her ears.

She started seeing the ex around corners, staring at her from across the street. Grant slept over most nights, but she still didn't feel safe. They couldn't call the police. Restraining orders were useless. On the night her ex followed her home, he'd grabbed her right arm and twisted, slowly, until she screamed and he let go, laughed and walked away. The x-ray revealed a cracked elbow. She'd packed with her left hand, her right arm cradled like a broken wing in a sling.

She couldn't win. Once again, she pulled out the boxes filled with crinkled paper, the corrugated cardboard to separate plates and bowls, the bubble wrap for wine glasses. She threw her daiquiri glasses on the wooden balcony, hearing the sharp crack as each stem separated from its bowl, and then stared at the splatter pattern of glass, a false barrier of protection. If he wanted, her ex could invade her life again. Nowhere was safe.

Whyte Noise

The last night in the apartment, Zoe watched the news on stolen cable. In a refugee camp in the Sudan, a mother cradled her starving child. The reporter said, "They've lost their farm, their livestock, their homes. Everything." If she wasn't so tired, she'd strike a match, burn the house down.

White-Out

T HE BUS ARRIVED LATE AT the Jubilee Auditorium and Zoe didn't get home from rehearsal until nearly midnight. Along the length of Whyte Avenue, the blue lights in the bare trees glittered. Plumes of exhaust rose straight up in the frosty air.

Grant was already in bed, covers pulled around his chin, watching *The Daily Show*.

"How was rehearsal?"

"Awful. The director keeps changing his mind about the staging in the second act." She chucked her skirt and sweater in the corner, hurried into her flannel pajamas, and crawled into bed, snuggling up next to his warmth.

"Cold hands," he complained. After a pause, he said, "Aunt Thelma died."

"Who?"

"My great-aunt. The funeral is Saturday afternoon. In Calgary."

"I have rehearsal Saturday night."

"Yeah, I know. I'm sorry." Grant slid his hand under her hair, massaging the knots in her shoulders. "We could drive down on Friday and leave after the funeral. It would mean a lot to my mom if we show up. You'd be back in time."

She didn't want to go to a funeral. But she owed him; he'd gone to her father's funeral in November. And met her mother. What type of portent was this for their relationship — meeting the family at funerals? At least she had a black dress.

They arrived in Calgary late Friday night. Grant's parents lived in a 1950s bungalow in the north-west quadrant of the city.

"You're late." Grant's mother gave him a quick hug. "I thought you'd make it for supper."

"I didn't get off work until five. And the roads were awful."

"You should have phoned."

Zoe stood uncomfortably in the back entrance, her mittens and hat dripping with wet snow. She held her coat in one hand until Grant took it from her and slung it over a kitchen chair.

"Mom, this is Zoe Willis," Grant said, deflecting his mother's attention away from himself. "This is my mom."

She was a short woman, much shorter than Zoe, dressed in a dark-brown suit. Drab brown hair cut in a short bob. Her face was square and white, with small brown eyes peering out. "Call me Shelia." The words were friendly, but the eyes weren't. They were appraising, summing up Zoe's worth and coming up a few zeros short.

Zoe bent to unlace her boots. Usually they made her feel confident, the square heels, the silver buckles at the calves shining aggressively. Now she felt like a biker chick crashing a bridge party. She wanted to say, *I'm not that person.* Whoever it was his mother saw. But maybe she was. Maybe she'd been deceiving herself about her worth all this time.

The kitchen was a dark cave, curtains shutting out the storm outside. Zoe sat down at the table, uncertain what she was expected to do.

"Let me get you some tea," Sheila said. "Unless you prefer coffee?"

"Tea is fine."

"So where are you from, Zoe?" she asked as she poured tea into a set of Esso stoneware, with pictures of Calgary landmarks etched on the side. The Zoo. The Calgary Tower.

Where was she from? All over, growing up in Germany and Ontario, university in British Columbia, and then teaching in Korea for two years. Two years in Vancouver after that. But she wasn't going to tell Grant's mother about her past.

"Right now, I'm from Edmonton."

"But where do your parents live?"

"My mother lives in Nelson."

"Are your parents divorced?" It felt like being interviewed by Oprah. Maybe she should have said, "In Nelson, Sheila," but she couldn't bring herself to call Grant's mother by her name.

"My dad died last year."

She saw the surprise, quickly masked. His mother thinking, *She can't be that old.* Zoe didn't offer any further details.

"I'm very sorry to hear that. Are you the only child?" Fishing for details. Was she the youngest, was she a trailer, was she years older than Grant? Zoe felt like yanking her chain, claiming to be forty. Hadn't Grant told his parents anything about her?

"I have an older brother."

"And you moved to Edmonton last summer. Was that for school?"

Grant interrupted. "Zoe had some problems with her last boyfriend. I told you that."

Squirming under the scrutiny, Zoe knew herself to be unworthy, a tainted woman trailing past relationships like cheap perfume.

"I'm in the music program at the U of A," she offered. Anything to stop the questions. "I'm doing my master's degree."

"In piano?

"No, voice. I sing opera."

"Opera. Well, that's different." Not very practical.

"She's a member of the Edmonton Opera Chorus," Grant boasted. He would tell this to anyone, people at work, strangers he met. "They're doing *Bohème*."

"I'm just in the chorus," Zoe was glad that Grant was standing up for her but oddly embarrassed. "I'm one of the street people." She was making things worse.

"Well," said Sheila. "How interesting." She checked her watch. "Visiting hours end at nine. We should get going."

"I didn't think we'd go tonight," Grant said. "I'm beat from the drive."

"Oh, you have to go. It wouldn't look right to miss visiting hours."

Ten minutes later, they were following Grant's parents south along Shaganappi Trail. After insisting that Grant had to show up, that his cousin would be insulted if he didn't, Sheila had wondered whether it was sensible to take an extra car, but Grant had won that point. Zoe stayed quiet. More than anything, she wished that they could afford a motel, but even the cheap ones in Calgary were over $100 a night.

The funeral home was a concrete building in the south-west. In a sterile reception area with a grey carpet, two huge arrangements of white mums and lilies stood like attendants.

They followed Grant's parents, turning right into a room that smelled of lemon furniture polish, overlaid with a bitter note of embalming fluid. Just inside the door stood a couple in their forties, the man in a black suit, the woman in an incongruous pink blouse and a long blue skirt. Zoe shook their hands, barely hearing the introductions. Wooden pews lined either side of an aisle with a red carpet. At the end was the open casket, with fuchsia curtains looped back with tasselled cords on either side.

The great-aunt wore a black crepe dress with a shiny butterfly brooch pinned at the shoulder. Her crossed hands were speckled with large brown spots. Skin like a crumpled moth. Unable to stop herself, Zoe reached out and touched the cold hand.

The cloying perfume of lilies permeated the room. Zoe swayed, images spilling across her mind. Her father in ICU, his face drained, the cheeks sunken like a papier-mâché mask. The respirator with its automatic timed breaths: *whoosh, click, whoosh, click.* In, out, in, out.

Her knees buckled. Grant grabbed her elbow to hold her up. "Are you okay?"

"I need to go outside." She could feel Sheila's disapproval pulsing towards her.

Snow was falling on the blue spruces clustered outside the entrance. Zoe took a deep breath, the icy air a slap to her face.

"It's like the scene with Mimi and Rudolpho. *Your little hand is cold.* Her hand was so cold." She was babbling, her mind skittering away from the edge of nothingness. They'd had a closed casket at her father's funeral. But the smell of the funeral home was the same.

Grant squeezed her hand, his fingers warm and comforting. She held on tight. "I don't think I can go back in. Can we leave?"

That night she curled up alone in a single bed. She'd been given the guest bedroom, two single beds with crocheted white spreads, white sheets, white shag carpet, white walls. In this blank space her mind whirred, a film projector ratcheting over images she couldn't control. Her father in a hospital bed, his skin as white as the walls. Her mother shivering uncontrollably in the private room when the doctor gave them the news. Her brother hadn't visited once.

She'd read a piece in *Wired* a few weeks earlier. A man in France had stolen $1.4 billion of art from museums. A Breughel painting: *Cheat Profiting from His Master.* A Watteau drawing, a seventeenth-century violin. Stashes of medieval weapons. He had stored them in his mother's house. Canvases stacked in his tiny bedroom. Ivory statues hidden in a wardrobe. When the man was arrested, his mother chopped up the paintings with a stolen axe and threw them in the Rhine-Rhone canal.

Zoe imagined the pictures floating slowly to the bottom of the murky canal, water seeping into the canvases. The utter waste of it all.

Her life reminded her of that story.

She woke up, smelling coffee and bacon. Zoe lay still for a moment, her head stuffy from the lack of sleep. Eight o'clock. Seven more hours of being polite. The funeral was at two and the wake after that. By three, four at the latest, they would be on their way home.

Grant's father had his face hidden behind the *Calgary Herald*. Zoe sidled into a chair beside Grant.

"Just coffee for me, please." Should she get it herself? Or would Sheila resent this?

"Oh, you need more than that. Let me make you some eggs."

"No, please, don't go to any trouble." She was hoping to stop at the Tims on the way to the funeral and pick up a blueberry muffin.

"We have cereal, if you prefer."

"No, thank you. Just coffee." Why didn't Grant say something, instead of just sitting there, forking in mouthfuls of egg?

Sheila set down a cup of coffee, and then sat down herself. "I was thinking, Zoe. You're a singer, aren't you? Well, maybe you could sing something at the funeral. Aunt Thelma loved "Amazing Grace". Do you know it?"

Her mind blanked. She couldn't think of an excuse.

"Would her family want me to sing?" she finally said.

"That's why I'm asking. I talked it over with Dan last night and told him you're a singer."

Zoe nodded. Dan must be the man she'd met at the funeral home.

"Umm, okay." She knew she sounded ungracious, but she didn't know how she could go back into that funeral home and keep her composure.

On the drive over, she asked Grant, "Why did your mother put me on the spot like that?"

"What do you mean?"

"Arranging for me to sing without even asking me first."

"You know the song, don't you?"

"Of course I do. I've sung it at funerals before. But I don't know the accompanist. I need to practice."

"She thought it would be a nice gesture. I think she was trying to include you." He was staring straight ahead, not looking at her. He sounded unconvinced by his own argument.

"I don't think I can sing right now. I'll mess it up."

"No one will care how you sing."

She cared. She shut up and looked out the window. Snow covered the sidewalks in front of the strip malls, softening their inherent ugliness.

At the next red light, Grant put his hand on her thigh. "Don't be mad."

"I'm not mad."

The funeral was in the same room as the night before. About forty people crowded into the back pews, avoiding the front like schoolchildren in a classroom. Zoe and Grant sat in a corner next to a woman whose rayon skirt spread over the seat. Looking around at the white heads, Zoe saw that she and Grant were the youngest people there, except for Dan's two teenagers, sitting forlornly in the front pew with their parents.

The minister had that ubiquitous haircut, short on the side with a floppy brown wave over the forehead. He stuttered over Thelma's name and didn't seem to know any details of her life. As he prayed that Thelma would be graciously received by the Lord, Zoe wondered if the great-aunt had believed any of this. She didn't know what she herself believed.

Memory grabbed her again, the ICU waiting room with its grey low-backed couches and the TV constantly turned to CBC news. Nights drinking stale coffee. Whispering promises over and over. Let him live. I'll switch to a sensible career, so he can be proud of me. I'll stay away from losers, date a normal guy, so he can stop worrying. She didn't know just whom she was making those promises to. She hadn't kept any of them, unless Grant counted as normal. She reached over and squeezed his hand.

Dan came to the pulpit to give the eulogy. He spoke of his mother's famous hospitality, inviting twenty people for Thanksgiving dinner, her love of quilting, her practical jokes, her sense of humour. Zoe looked at the program, with its white dove on the front cover and the picture inside of the great-aunt in a blue dress, smiling a big toothy grin.

She'd been here and now she was gone.

The minister was back at the pulpit. "And now, Zoe Willis will sing Thelma's favourite song, 'Amazing Grace'."

He'd pronounced her last name wrong, making her sound like one of the crazy dead women from *Giselle*. As if she'd dance a man to death for betraying her.

She walked to the front. "Give me a four-bar entry," she whispered to the organist. Her throat felt tight with nerves. She should have brought a bottle of water. The pitch on the organ sounded high.

She sang the first three lines of "Amazing Grace". Feeling the quaver in the fourth line, she tried to push through, lost control of her breath, and swallowed the final "see". If only the organist would play a little faster.

Her mind blanked on the third verse. She'd sung the song a hundred times, but she couldn't remember the words. The organist started into the chords, recognized her problem, and improvised a solo, adding trills and bridges. Under the cover of the music, he whispered, "Through many dangers, toils, and snares." The words flooded back, and she came in on the entry as if the interlude had been planned.

As the mourners filed out after the coffin, Zoe went up to speak with the organist, a small balding man with a trim mustache. "Thanks for the save," she said. "I don't know what happened. I've sung 'Amazing Grace' before."

"Think nothing of it." He waved his right hand dismissively through the air. "I play for funerals all the time. Most of the singers are amateurs."

Zoe smiled weakly. After the way she'd performed, she couldn't protest that she wasn't an amateur. The adrenaline of performance had ebbed, leaving her shaky with exhaustion. Only the wake to get through.

Grant hugged her shoulders. "You did great, hon." No one else commented. Shelia avoided them.

At four, Zoe stood with Grant at the back door of his parents' house. The sun was already setting though a haze of blowing snow, a weak yellow glow.

"We should get going," Grant said to his mother. "We'll be driving in the dark as it is."

Zoe stood beside him, frantic with impatience. Practice started at 7:30. She'd been pushing Grant to leave since 3:30, but his mother had insisted they come back for coffee.

"Why don't you stay," Sheila asked. "It's Saturday night. You don't have to work tomorrow."

Zoe glanced over at Grant. He wasn't saying anything. "I have to be at rehearsal by 7:30."

"The roads will be terrible, Zoe. It's been snowing all day. And I don't want to drive in the dark. Couldn't you miss rehearsal, just this once?" His brow was wrinkled, that implacable look that said she was being unreasonable, that he knew better. A flat stubbornness.

"No, I can't. I have to show up." She couldn't believe her tone. She sounded like a prima donna. Really, she just couldn't stand another hour with Grant's mother.

"Fine, okay." Grant turned to his mother. "I guess we have to get going."

"Well, it was nice meeting you." Sheila clearly hoped that it would be the last time. "Be careful driving back."

Grant waited until they were in the car before speaking. "Why do you always do that?"

"What?"

"Make your life more important than mine."

"You said we'd be back in time for rehearsal."

"I didn't know the weather would be so bad. Would it kill you to stay another night?" He fiddled with the dash controls, cold air blasting through the vents. "Look at it coming down."

She said nothing. Sometimes he made her so angry she couldn't speak. There was no room for compromise with him. He always thought he was right.

"Fine. Have it your way." He got out of the car to scrape the ice off the windshield.

By the time they reached Airdrie, the sun had set. The long tunnel of the road, lit by headlights, was pitted with ruts of ice and snow. On the right hand, the darkened ditch waited. A truck loomed behind them, headlights illuminating the snow swirling around them, a tungsten glare. Grant slowed to fifty. The truck careened past in the fast lane, sending waves of gravel and snow over the windscreen. Zoe grabbed the side handle, bracing herself.

Another truck slid by them in a whoosh of snow. The Sentra bucked and rocked, caught in the backdraft. Grant gripped the steering wheel, his knuckles white.

"Can't we pull over?"

"We'd slide into the ditch."

A single tail light appeared in front of them, a motorcycle or a car with a broken light. All she could see was the red glow, like a warning or a stop sign.

"Look out!"

"Shit." He took his foot off the gas, but the car was right in front of them, half in their lane and half on the shoulder, a long black car with a low bumper, the single tail light gleaming like an evil eye. Grant swerved into the passing lane and the tires slid on a patch of black ice, pulling them towards the opposite ditch.

She'd heard that in an accident your life flashed before your eyes. She didn't have time to think. Grant cranked the wheel in the direction of the skid. Halogen beams illuminated those few seconds, the skid to the left, the wheels sliding under them, the windshield wipers whipping madly back and forth.

The tires hit ruts of packed snow, jarred the car sideways, then caught and corrected, pulling the car back to the middle of the road. Grant eased them over to the slow lane, crawling to twenty.

"Fucking asshole! What the hell was he thinking, stopping like that?" Sweat slickened his forehead. "We're turning around at the next overpass."

On the drive back to Calgary, Zoe replayed those few moments over and over. The red tail light appearing out of the darkness. The slow slide towards the ditch. She felt frozen. Her fault, everything was her fault.

Neither of them spoke until they finally pulled up in front of the house. Then Grant turned off the ignition and leaned over, putting his hand on Zoe's thigh.

"Are you okay, hon?"

She nodded, shivering. "I'm sorry," she said. She wasn't sure why she was apologizing. She was sorry for all the flaws in her life. For all the problems that trailed after her like plumes of car exhaust on a winter night.

"I'll just tell Mom the roads were too icy." He didn't need to say they would avoid mentioning the near accident. Zoe knew she would be blamed if Sheila ever found out. She blamed herself. Every choice she made was wrong.

Zoe took a long hot shower and then went to bed. After what seemed like hours, she rolled over and checked the illuminated red glow of the clock radio. 2:15. Nights of insomnia had taught her coping mechanisms: get out of bed, read a detective novel, drink a cup of peppermint tea, watch a late-night movie. Anything to distract her from the night terrors. Maybe she could tuck herself into bed with Grant in his bedroom, a childhood sanctuary still decorated with Bruce Lee posters and Star Wars memorabilia.

He was her hot-water bottle when she couldn't sleep, on the nights when worries about her ex stalking her in Edmonton, her mother alone in Nelson, her increasing student loans, and her stalled career buzzed along the nerve endings, truths she couldn't ignore in the dark. At three in the morning, she'd try to visualize the next year and see a fuzzy TV screen, grey and indistinct. She'd stare at the ceiling, the same thoughts repeating over and over in her head. Then she'd roll over and slide her hand along the comforting curve of Grant's stomach. Feel it lift and fall, listening to the slight wheeze of his breathing.

Zoe pulled on her track pants. Her door creaked as she slowly opened it. She paused, but no one stirred. She tiptoed down the hall towards Grant's room. Her hand was on the doorknob when Sheila opened the opposite door, clutching a green terrycloth robe tight at the neck.

"I heard a noise. Do you need something? Another blanket? A glass of water?"

Sheila stared her down, daring her to make a move.

Zoe wanted to ask, *Who do you think I am? You know nothing about me.* But she was afraid of the answer. Whoever she was wouldn't be good enough. There was nothing that she could say that would make Sheila accept her.

She opened the door to Grant's room, went in, and closed the door behind her. A streetlight shone through the blinds, casting orange stripes on the wall. She lifted the comforter and crawled into the single bed. Grant rolled over and she nestled against his back. Placing her hand on his stomach, she breathed slowly, in and out.

Dancing the Requiem

THE BALLET IS MOZART FOR a modern age, dancers marching in khaki fatigues, machine guns held in clenched fists; dancers dressed as Afghan women in full blue hijab, their faces covered with veils, mourning the dead. A requiem for the Canadian soldiers killed in Afghanistan, but also a prayer for peace. Zoe watches the troupe come offstage after rehearsal, their inward intense focus. Friendly but distant, living in their pack, a group of teenagers mostly, all with beautiful toned bodies and fanatical dedication. Like soldiers, their lives dedicated to a cause.

The chorus stands behind the stage arranged in giant open boxes, like grouping of vases in an IKEA display. On the monitor is the conductor, down in the music pit. In front of them, facing the audience, is Mozart, a Japanese dancer in an eighteenth-century white frock coat and breeches. His wig glitters with silver. His feet are fastened to the podium as if he is emerging from its stone base, a statue brought to life. He sways forward, almost level to the stage, then to the side, bending at impossible angles and then righting himself.

"He looks like he's wearing ski boots," Rachel whispers to Zoe.

"Shh." Their cue is coming up.

Introit Requiem

Count Franz von Walsegg commissioned a requiem mass after the death of his wife, Anna, on February 14, 1791. In July, Walsegg had intermediaries approach Mozart secretly. He planned to pass the work off as his own, as he had done with other composers' work.

The dancers have been given the dressing rooms behind the main stage, with the chorus relegated to the basement dressing rooms. Zoe doesn't mind, although a few of the more prima donna types, like Pria, gripe about the conductor *favouring* the members of Alberta Ballet Company in what was supposed to a *collaboration* between the two companies. She doesn't say this around the conductor, just in the bar afterwards.

Backstage, they slip out of their brown monks' robes. "Not much of a costume this time," Rachel complains. "At least it's not a Merry Widow in a size six. I could barely take a breath in *La Traviata*. Those hoop skirts weighed ten pounds."

Zoe loves the costumes, the make-up, the disguise. Even in these coarse robes, her hair pulled harshly back in a bun, she feels transformed, outside of the ordinary world. In jeans and a T-shirt, she feels awkward and conspicuous. Lately, her jeans have been pulling even tighter at the waistband and fat rolls spill over either side of her brassiere. She is still a size 10, but just barely. Too many meals cooked for two, steaks on the barbeque with a side of baked potato and sour cream, turkey lasagna with tomato sauce smothering handfuls of grated cheese and cottage cheese, rich pork goulash with egg noodles and white buns to sop up the gravy.

"Coming out for a drink?" Rachel asks. She's left her stage makeup on, her vivid blue eyes outlined in thick streaks of black kohl, heavy lines of blush accentuating her cheekbones. Rachel lusts after James, a scruffy six-foot tenor with a wispy beard, and never misses an opportunity to flirt with him when the chorus goes to the Black Dog after rehearsals.

"I better not. Grant has to be at work early tomorrow."

"Come on, Zoe. Just because you're living together doesn't mean you have to act all married. Just one drink. Please?" Rachel clasps her hands together. "I hate going on my own."

The Black Dog on Whyte sits above an Indian restaurant. Upstairs, the dark room stinks of stale beer. The eight members of the chorus crowd around one of the long tables at the back, near the bathrooms.

Zoe twirls her glass of red wine, listening to Pria and Rachel argue over the lead soprano's voice. She'd checked the soprano's résumé; she always checked. Where had she done her training, what roles had she played, what awards had she won? What was she paid? Zoe knows that several of the soloists are billeted with Edmonton families; the cost of hotels isn't covered by the opera company and the soloists couldn't afford a month in a hotel each time they took a role.

Chorus members make about $500 per opera. Zoe worked out the hourly rate once: $30 an hour for performances, $5 an hour for dress rehearsals, and $2 an hour for practices. She makes more money at her afternoon waitressing shift at the Urban Diner, even before tips. She is still paying off the credit card debt her ex racked up in Vancouver. VISA doesn't care that she hadn't made the purchases.

As if her thoughts have conjured an apparition, she notices a man sitting at a table by the stairway, at the front of the room. Brown hair in a ponytail. Thick belligerent shoulders. His back is to her, and she can't tell for certain, but something about the man's pose reminds her of her ex.

Zoe hunches down, feeling trapped. She knows it is ridiculous to feel so frightened when she has other people around her, but panic pounds in her head. "I should get home. Can you walk me to my car?" she asks James.

"Are you going already?" Rachel pouts, but for once Zoe isn't vulnerable to guilt-tripping. After a few minutes of arguing, Rachel comes along, pretending to need fresh air. Zoe walks out of the bar between them, trying to hide behind James' height.

The car is parked two blocks over, and with each block Zoe feels her anxiety grow, that prickly feeling between her shoulder blades. She resists looking behind her; she can barely focus when Rachel asks if she'll give her a ride to practice the next night. Inside the car, Zoe slams the button on the door locks even before she puts her key in the ignition.

Grant is in bed when she slips into the room. "Sorry I'm late," she says.

"Yeah, well, I have to get up early." He rolls away from her, burrowing his head under the covers.

Zoe reaches over tentatively, slipping a hand under his T-shirt, touching the soft, warm flesh of his stomach. "Don't be mad." She needs the security of his arms. "Rachel wanted me to come along." Sliding her hand under the elastic of his boxer shorts, she rubs the muscle along his thigh.

"You always drink too much when you go out with the chorus."

"I only had a glass of wine. I'm a cheap drunk," she teases. Finally, he rolls towards her, kisses her, his tongue brushing her lips, adding his salty taste to the red wine infusing her mouth.

Zoe is chopping red peppers when her phone rings. "Can you grab that?"

Grant glances at the call display. "It's a pay phone." He picks up the cell phone, listens without a comment, and hands it over to Zoe. "It's your brother."

"Hi, Steve." She cradles the phone between her shoulder and neck. "Yeah, I'm just making supper. Okay. Okay. Sure, we'll get you." She hangs up, keeping her back turned away from Grant, preparing for an argument. "Steve just came in on the bus. I said we'd pick him up."

"Does he have a place to stay?"

"I doubt it. Maybe he could sleep on the couch again." She tosses the peppers in the pan, adding a dollop of sweet soy and some ginger out of a jar, focusing on the veggies sizzling in the pan.

"Did you tell him not to invite his friends over this time?"

"You heard me on the phone. I just invited him for supper."

"Which will turn into inviting him to stay and he'll still be here in a week."

She pulls the skin off a garlic bulb, minces the garlic, and throws it in with the peppers. "Last time was different." The oil smokes. Zoe turns on the fan, avoiding Grant's gaze.

"Don't you have rehearsal tonight?" Grant asks.

"Yes. I'm sorry. I didn't know what to say." She tosses the veggies, turns off the heat, and sets the pan to the back of the stove. "We should get going. He's waiting at the station."

Steve had stayed with them in early December. He'd shown up a month after the funeral. He went out every night and came home drunk. Twice he brought buddies back with him. Grant kept telling her to put her foot down, but she'd never been able to tell her brother anything. Finally, on December 22, Zoe drove them both to Nelson to spend Christmas with their mother. She left Steve there.

Steve is waiting outside the bus depot, his hockey bag dumped on the ground. Grant grimaces as Steve slings the bag into the trunk of the Nissan Sentra, the wet bottom thwacking against the clean carpet.

Her brother's look hasn't changed since the late nineties: long shaggy black hair, a black leather jacket patterned with silver studs. He has a small goatee, like a line of dirt extending down from his sideburns. He climbs into the back seat and immediately puts his foot on her seatbelt, the way he'd done on car rides when they were kids. Pulling the seatbelt away from her neck, Zoe snaps, "Move your foot."

"How's the *yo-de-lah-hee-hing*?" He always does this, drawling the word, mocking opera's pretensions.

"Good," Zoe says shortly. "I'm in rehearsals for *Requiem*. How's your music going?"

"Some guys asked me to play backup on this demo. They're shopping it around."

"Did you get paid?" Whether he was paid or not is irrelevant. He makes more on EI from his summer construction work than she does from her part-time waitressing job and her opera pay combined.

Kyrie Eleison

Mozart was paid 100 ducats, a first installment on the *Requiem*. During the summer of 1791, he finished two operas, *La Clemenza di Tito* and *The Magic Flute*. By November he was ill, believing he'd been poisoned. He would never finish *Requiem*. Death was dancing towards him.

Monday is the first full rehearsal with orchestra. Zoe sits in a chair next to Rachel, waiting for Courtney, the makeup artist with green streaks in her short hair and a mermaid tattoo. Rachel pulls her long hair back into a bun and pushes in bobby pins.

"Have you decided whether to audition for next year?"

"Not yet." Grant wants her to try some other career. Something practical. "I could ask Tim to leave," he said. "I know he drives you crazy. But I can't carry this place on my own, not with the taxes due in June. The utility bills doubled last year. If you found a better job, we could even fix up the kitchen."

She has read that the Alberta Ballet Company dancers are paid around $15,000 a year. Not enough for a one-bedroom apartment, not with rents jumping over 10% in the last year to over a thousand a month. If she weren't living with Grant, she'd be struggling.

She could follow the dream her entire life and never reach it. The dancers have one chance. If they aren't good enough at twenty, they'll never be good enough. But she could still be singing in the chorus at fifty. Is that what she wants?

Confutatis

Soldiers in fatigues circle the stage around the platform where Mozart conducts, the music gripping him with such power that he sways backwards, knees bent, almost falling, anchored to the ground yet always reaching for the notes that dance in his mind. The soldiers push the platform across the stage, transforming it into a bunker, a shelter from enemy fire.

"Tenors, you're behind on the eighth bar entry. Again, from *Confutatis maledictis*." The conductor hums a few notes. He knows the entire score in Latin in addition to the orchestration. This level of knowledge is beyond her.

Everyone knows who the future stars are. The golden boy. They all hear it in his voice. That something extra. In the MFA program, he landed all the plum roles: Papageno in *The Magic Flute*, the "Au Fond du Temple Saint" duet from Bizet's *The Pearl Fishers*, the title role in *Faust*. The golden baritone. He will go far.

She waits until she's back from rehearsal to tackle Steve. Grant is watching a movie with Tim, his downstairs tenant. Steve has spread the contents of his duffel bag over Grant's recliner in the living room, jeans and shirts heaped on the seat, jacket tossed over the back. Zoe drags in a wooden chair from the kitchen. In passing, she notes the encrusted bowls piled in the sink, the splatters of spaghetti sauce on the stove, the empty milk carton on the counter. Steve hasn't washed a dish in the three days he's been here. Living in a house with two guys, Zoe is always resisting the urge to clean.

"So what are you doing here?"

"I need a break from Lindsay. She's pregnant."

"Steve." Zoe sighs the name out, like the hiss of air out of a bicycle tire. "What are you going to do?"

"Dunno. It's my kid. I think."

"Are you sure?"

Steve flashes a smile at her, replete with the sly charm that still gets him women, even if he can't hold a job. "Hey, that's a guy's line. Aren't you supposed to be a feminist?"

Her brother's life is a Puccini opera: characters blinded by passion doing the stupidest things, always optimistic even as life beats them down. She can map the next ten years, the flush of optimism after the child is born, backsliding, custody fights, missed child support payments, her mother trying to maintain contact because it might be her grandchild. Her mother says that Steve just needs time, he'll grow up. Zoe gave up on him years ago.

"Grant's a good guy. Better than that last loser."

She can't argue. But is it enough to be with a "good guy"?

"You know, you should visit Mom more this summer," Steve says. "Make sure she's okay. I don't think she's coping well."

"Why me?" Zoe asks. "I'm in school, remember."

"Yeah, but you don't have a job or a lease. I can't leave my apartment."

"Well, maybe you should get back to that apartment. Anyway, I do have a job. Two jobs." He always shuffles off any responsibility. He didn't come to the hospital after their dad had a stroke; he didn't stay after the funeral. Zoe helped their mother with all the arrangements: the funeral, the lawyer, the meeting with the insurance agent. She has driven back to Nelson twice since December, terrified by the icy roads in the Kicking Horse Pass. But Steve is right — their mother isn't coping well. The last time Zoe was there, her mother spent the entire weekend in a bathrobe.

At three in the morning, there's a loud thumping on the front door. Zoe gets up and puts on her track pants. Grant pulls a pillow over his head.

"Hey, little sister." Steve leans against the railing on the front porch, his jacket open, his eyes bloodshot.

"Shh," Zoe says, pulling him inside. "Grant's asleep." Actually, Grant is awake and furious. She helps Steve unlace his boots and guides him into the living room.

Steve falls onto the sofa. Zoe hovers for a minute, wondering if he is drunk enough to fall asleep immediately or if he'll want to talk and be impossible to shut up. She doesn't want Grant to come out and start yelling.

"Where were you?" she asks. She doesn't really want to know. She doesn't know what to say to Steve anymore. She doesn't know who he is.

"Somewhere. I had to get out."

"You can't keep doing this. I have first dress rehearsal tomorrow. I need some sleep."

Her brother covers his eyes with his right hand. He is crying. "I know I wasn't there. I couldn't go to the hospital. I'm sorry. I'm sorry."

Zoe sits down beside him. She wants to cry, but she can't. She couldn't cry at the hospital either, when her mother broke down. She could only sit there, holding her mother's hand.

Steve stops crying after a few minutes. "Sorry," he says hoarsely, rubbing his eyes with the back of his hand. Zoe gets him a Kleenex, and then helps him take off his jacket. He lies down and she covers him with a blanket.

Back in the bedroom, she crawls into bed. Grant rolls over and pulls her close. "He leaves today," he says. "I'll check the bus schedules and drive him to the station. Does he have enough money for the ticket?"

Zoe says nothing. She's shaken. Her brother didn't cry at their father's funeral either. She doesn't think she's ever seen him cry.

She gives Grant her Wednesday night dress rehearsal pass. Their last chance to get everything right. The tenors still haven't memorized the words for the *Offertorium*. In the *Agnus Dei* section, two dancers collided, ruining the intricate choreography.

She takes a deep breath, waiting for her cue. The male dancers wait offstage, the trio of death who will circle the trio of life. She loves watching this, the quick costume changes, the outlined muscles drenched with sweat, the brief moments when the mask of performance drops and the panting human beings emerge.

Domine Hostia

Three women dressed in white: a pregnant woman, a mother holding her baby, an old woman. Three demons in masks enter. The lead dancer in the trio displays the chiselled abs of a body builder. When he moves, she believes in possession. On stage, he becomes Death, his dark mask obscuring his features, moving with menace towards the young mother cradling her child. Death attacking life. Will the baby behave itself tonight? At the matinée dress rehearsal, he'd screamed when the devil swooped him offstage, held high above his head. The junior high students roared approval.

Grant meets her at the back door of the Jubilee afterwards. Rain is spitting down on the pavement and the air smells of wet dirt and fresh grass. To the northwest, storm clouds pile up in wet grey clumps. Grant has dressed up. Zoe had warned him that the Directors' Circle members, big contributors to the opera, would be attending the wine and cheese reception.

She doesn't get to see him in his dress pants and his midnight blue shirt very often. Most days he wears black jeans and a sweater to work. She runs her fingers up the soft cotton sleeves of his shirt, slipping a hand around the back of his neck, wishing Pria or one of the other snottier chorus members would come out and see him.

"What did you think?"

"I kept thinking of *Amadeus*. When Mozart is dying and Salieri keeps saying, 'You go too fast, you go too fast.' The food at the reception was great. Stuffed figs and pork shish kebabs. Plus wine. It's too bad the chorus couldn't go."

"Did you see me?" She wants affirmation, approval.

"Yeah, second from the left in the upper box, next to that really large woman. It wasn't a very flattering costume."

She can't believe that all he noticed is her costume. "We're supposed to blend with the background. The dancers are the focus." She doesn't like who she is becoming with him. She doesn't want to be this person, always worried about money, always feeling inadequate.

"This is what I love. You don't understand."

"I want you to do what makes you happy."

She pulls back. "You say that and yet you complain all the time that I don't have any money. Pay more rent, pay the taxes, get a better job. What do you really want? Do you want me to quit singing? Is that it?"

Looking at him, his face set in a stubborn frown, Zoe thinks, *Will we be having the same fight in a year, in ten years, twenty?* The uncertainty of her future terrifies her. She wants a coda, a sign that this is the ending, that everything will be resolved.

Lacrimosa

Mozart died on December 5, 1791. His widow, Constanze, asked Joseph von Eybler and then Franz Xaver Süssmayr to finish the music, but did it secretly so that she could collect the remaining portion of the commission. Süssmayr composed part of the music for the *Lacrimosa* section and added *Sanctus*, *Beneditus* and *Agnes Dei*.

The tax bill arrives on Friday. Zoe refuses to pay half. "It's your house. If we split up, you'd have the house and I'd have nothing. I pay rent and half the utilities. Why should I pay more?"

"Great. I'm stuck with all the responsibility. Opera is so fucking impractical. What if I'd chosen a career with no future?"

"You didn't have to fucking choose!"

She slams the door on her way out of the house. No future. He'd hit her sore spot. That's what happens in a relationship — you let someone in close enough to hurt you.

Half an hour later, she is at the Starbucks on Whyte Avenue with Rachel. She orders a decaf latte with skim, feeling guilty because the drink costs five dollars. She can't even order a coffee without considering the cost.

"He wants me to pay half the house taxes. It's not my fucking house."

"He is so controlling," Rachel agrees.

"And not supportive at all. Do you know what he said after the dress rehearsal? He said, and I quote, 'Do people really like this stuff?'"

But even as she is ranting, the familiar refrain of misunderstandings, Zoe thinks, *He did come to the dress rehearsal.* Does he have to like opera for the relationship to work?

Would she be happier with or without him? Should she even be asking this question?

"I don't know what to do after next year," she confesses. "I don't even know if I want to stay in this shitty city. But he has a good job here."

Zoe sips her coffee and the liquid hits her soft palate, scorching it. For the next week she has a coin-sized burn on the top of her mouth, a constant irritant, her tongue drawn to the bubbled blister of skin.

After the Saturday night performance, the chorus goes for drinks at the University Earls. Zoe gulps two quick glasses of red wine. Her performance high is ebbing and she wants to hold on to the excitement. She doesn't want to go home. She hasn't spoken to Grant since the fight the day before.

Earls is dimly lit, loud with conversation. Rachel is on the other side of the table, leaning towards James, all her attention centred on him. Her filmy red top brushes against his bare arm. Zoe watches the choreography of attraction, feeling apart from everything, in a bubble. The music of the *Requiem* echoes in her head: *Confutatis, Benedictus*. Deep baritones and the high counterpoint of the sopranos. The dancers in devil masks circling the women in white. The trio of death.

Zoe gets up and the world shifts. The bathrooms are downstairs, down a poorly lit set of stairs and around a corner, next to the kitchen. She walks carefully, holding on to the rail. The last thing she needs to do is twist her ankle.

She sits in the stall for several minutes, cradling her chin in her hands, her head spinning. No one will miss her.

As she opens the door, she sees her ex leaning up against the wall by the door, his arms crossed against his black leather jacket. He smiles but says nothing.

Zoe freezes. Does she go back into the stall? But that door offers no protection. She walks by him quickly, not stopping to wash her hands. As she passes, her ex reaches out and shoves her, hard, against the nearest sink. Her hip bashes against the porcelain. Zoe stumbles, catches her balance, grabs the handle of the door, and flings herself out into corridor.

She runs up the stairs. He won't follow. He's had his fun.

It isn't until she sits down that she starts trembling. Her back is to the stairs; she won't know when he leaves. Her bubble shattered, leaving her exposed.

She'd had a restraining order against him in Vancouver. When she moved to Edmonton, he followed her. There would never be an ending.

Communion

Mozart was buried in an unmarked grave. On December 10, 1791, the opening sections of the *Requiem* were performed at

St Michael's Church in a memorial for Mozart. The completed *Requiem* was delivered to Count Franz von Walsegg in 1792 with Mozart's forged signature.

A week after the last performance, her mom phones.

"Steve's been charged with a DUI. He lost his license and his truck has been impounded. Can you come home, just for a week or so?"

Grant doesn't ask when she will be back. They avoid the topic. Zoe packs a suitcase and her laptop. She asks for a week off at work, even though she needs the money and tips from the summer hours to pay part of her fall tuition.

She hasn't told Grant about the attack at Earls. What could he do? She has stopped confiding in him. With rehearsals, performances, and work at the restaurant, she has barely seen him in the last month. She once thought that everything would work out. Since her father's death, she no longer believes that.

She leaves Thursday morning. The Trans-Canada through the Kicking Horse Pass is backed up with eighteen-wheelers and recreational vehicles. Smoke from a forest fire burning near Revelstoke fills the air, reducing visibility. Zoe's eyes water in the orange haze, and she grips the steering wheel as transport trucks shoot by her.

When she arrives in Nelson, she sits in the car for a moment outside her parents' house. Her mother's house. Patchy overgrown grass and purple petunias spilling out of terracotta pots on the front steps. A few roof tiles are peeling back. The house looks abandoned, the curtains closed. Her parents moved here after her dad retired: twenty-six years in the military. He'd lived in the house for just two years.

Her mother seemed more focused than she been during the last visit. She makes coffee and sits down with Zoe at the kitchen table. When Zoe visited in April, her mother had wandered around the kitchen, unable to sit down for more than five minutes.

"So what happened?" Zoe asks.

Her mother launches into a convoluted explanation: Steve was helping a friend build a fence, they had a couple of beers (Zoe doubts it was a couple), and Steve took a half-finished beer when he left. He was pulled over for speeding and tossed the can in the back seat. The cops smelled the beer, charged him with drunk driving and open liquor, and impounded his truck. Now Steve has a court date on Monday in Kelowna and needs someone to drive him.

"Why can't his girlfriend drive him to court?"

"Lindsay is eight months pregnant."

Steve hadn't told her that. He'd implied that the pregnancy was a new discovery.

The friend with the fence doesn't seem to be offering a ride. Zoe doesn't ask why her mother can't do it. Her mother always let her father do the driving. The car in the garage has probably only been driven as far as the grocery store and back in the last seven months.

There are people — her brother, her ex — who fuck up over and over and expect other people to solve the problems. And there are people — her father, Zoe — who pick up the pieces.

That night, she can't sleep. An orange streetlight casts parallel lines through the blinds of the spare room. She has spent too many nights in this room in the last year, staring at the ceiling.

At one in the morning, she pulls out her cell phone and texts Grant.

I miss you.

Five minutes later, he texts back. *I miss you too.*

It's a mess here. I miss my dad.

I'm sorry.

She didn't know if he is sorry about her dad, sorry about the mess her brother has made, or sorry about their latest fight. It doesn't matter.

I'll be back on Wednesday, she texts. She'll spend the weekend with her mother, cut the grass, and drive her brother to court. And then she will drive back. She didn't make this mess, and she's not cleaning it up.

How You Look at Things

WHEN RACHEL'S CELL PHONE RANG, she checked the number and mentally braced herself.

"Hi, Mom."

"What did you do with your father's golf clubs?"

"They're probably in the basement closet, where you always store them."

"They're not there. You took them, didn't you?"

"No, I didn't take the golf clubs." She had never played golf.

"You're getting rid of my things. The cranberry glasses are missing. And your father's hockey jacket."

"You gave the hockey jacket to Uncle Ted after Dad died."

"Why would I give away his jacket?"

Over the past two years, Rachel had noticed her mother's frequent confusion. Missing words, forgetfulness, fits of anger. The doctor had diagnosed early-onset dementia. Possibly Korsakoff's Syndrome.

Sitting at the Value Village table, its surface splashed with white and green paint, she half-listened to the familiar complaints: Sue, her mother's sister, is stealing her money, the bank is sending threatening letters. Nobody cares about her now.

"Have you seen your doctor this week?" Rachel asked. She'd learned to switch the subject whenever her mother became too worked up. She would speak slowly, one topic at a time. Her mother had already forgotten about the cranberry glasses, long broken. She'd forgotten about the golf clubs, gathering dust in the closet under the basement stairs.

After her mother finally hung up, Rachel ticked off each item on her list of chores. She'd worked her last shift at work, paid her roommate her share of the rent, and packed her clothes and books. Tomorrow morning, she was driving to Canmore for a day at the Folk Festival. Then Kelowna for the third time this year.

The last time she'd been at her mother's house, she'd spent a day cleaning the kitchen.

The Fridge

> *Ham slices, green with mould*
> *Opened cans of beans with jagged lids still attached*
> *Rotting heads of brown lettuce*
> *Expired salad dressing and mayonnaise*
> *Frozen meat encrusted with ice crystals*

She'd emptied the fridge, scrubbed it, and then sorted through the unopened bills stuffed in the bread box and piled on the ironing board. Some of the bills went back six months.

Things to Do

> *Pay the electricity for May and June*
> *Cut up VISA card / Check about $3100 unpaid balance*
> *Phone life insurance / Find out why Dad's claim hasn't been settled*
> *Talk to CPP about early withdrawals*

Did her mother have enough insurance money to last for the next twenty years? She hadn't worked for over thirty years. She wasn't eligible for OAS for another five years. Would she agree to sell the house?

Lying in bed, her eyes closed, Rachel added up the numbers. Working full-time at the Diner Deluxe for the spring and summer, she'd made $7,000, but most of it went to bills. If she moved to Kelowna, found a job, and lived with her mother, she could save money.

Budget for July

   $600 for ½ the rent
   $500 utilities and food
   $300 insurance and gas

In Bowness, she picked up Jazz, who worked with her at the diner. Rachel had mentioned she was going to the folk festival, and Jazz offered a tent in return for a drive. She was waiting with two other people in a yard thick with dandelions.

"This is Vikki and Joe." Vikki had spiky blonde hair and a jewelled belly ring glinting between orange tank-top and combat pants. Joe's chin sprouted a scruffy brown tuft, like a goat's beard. Rachel hadn't expected two extra passengers. The trunk was full of her stuff. Joe and Vikki had to squish into the back seat with the tent and luggage. They discussed Greg Brown and Janis Ian as Jazz leaned over the seat to talk to them.

In Canmore, Rachel dropped the others at the campground and left the car, walking over to Centennial Park to join a crowd of teenagers in hip huggers and white T-shirts; well-aged hippies with matted braids framing seamed faces, looking like

Hollywood extras from a Woodstock reunion; tanned hikers pulling huskies and labs. The park smelled of sun-warmed grass, fried doughnuts, lamb curry, and roasting coffee. Poplars glowed yellow in the August sun.

Once through the gate, she hurried for the right side of the stage, a cooler in her right hand and the tarp under her arm. Then her foot hit a tree root and she fell, sprawling, the tarp unfolding, the cooler falling on its side, spilling ice and bottles of water. A pratfall joke out of a silent movie.

"Jeez, there's ice all over my tarp." A woman spilling out of a wrap-around skirt and a volunteer's lime-green T-shirt glared at her.

Her right knee was bleeding. She'd bit her tongue, which felt swollen. "Sorry," she mumbled as she picked scattered bottles out of the pine needles.

"My blanket's all wet."

"I said I'm sorry." Rachel slammed the lid shut, scrunched the tarp into a ball, and stood up. Blood trickled slowly down her leg as she limped away.

Blue and orange tarps dotted the area in front of the Stan Rogers Stage; low lawn chairs sprouted like mushrooms. Retreating into the trees, Rachel spread the tarp on a lumpy spot of dirt and pegged down the four corners. The acrid smell of pot drifted from a group clustered near a clump of pine trees.

A couple of girls in long skirts began an impromptu dance, arms weaving patterns. A tiny woman, white-haired and bent, stood up. Rachel watched as the woman imitated the girls' moves, an old oak trying to sway with saplings in the breeze. Then the woman laughed and looked at Rachel, her eyes as bright blue as stained glass.

We had dances every weekend in the community hall. A French fiddler played reels. I was the best dancer. I could dance until dawn. All the men wanted me as a partner.

"Hello, Canmore." The voice boomed from the loudspeakers. Looking over at the stage, Rachel saw the woman in the skirt and lime-green shirt holding a microphone.

"How're you all feeling?" the woman bellowed. People whooped and clapped. "All right! Let's get ready to party."

The old woman spun around one more time and then smiled. *In the old days, everyone was happier.*

A chilly breeze blew over Rachel's shoulder. She shivered, wishing for a warm body beside her. Someone to lean against.

Two years ago, at the Vancouver Folk Festival, she and her ex had cuddled under a sleeping bag, sharing a thermos of Irish coffee, thick with Baileys and cream. Suddenly she longed for that smooth sugary taste

Standing in a long line for coffee, Rachel felt someone crowding her. Turning, she saw the woman in the lime-green shirt. Up close, she looked about forty-five, with the smooth skin of the overweight. A long braid of grey hair fell over her shoulder.

"I'm sorry again about your tarp," Rachel said.

The woman put a hand on her shoulder. "Hey, it's too beautiful here to be unhappy. Of course," she laughed, "I bought my condo before the boom. Paid a hundred thou and now it's worth three. Make your own luck, that's what I say."

Make your own luck was one of her mother's sayings. *Count your blessings.* She'd always worn rose-coloured glasses. Look what happened with rose-coloured glasses.

"My father died of a stroke last year," Rachel said flatly. "He was fifty-nine. Did he make his own luck?" She didn't want sympathy. She just needed to say the words.

Back at the tarp, she sipped her coffee, listening to a woman with an acoustic guitar and songs about relationships gone bad.

"I overheard this one in a New York coffee shop. Hope I don't jinx this great weather by singing about the rain." Chords rolled like water over stones in a deep creek. *"The rain is always falling, falling, falling."*

Rachel wiped tears away with the back of her hand. For the past two years, she'd been falling.

A voice harsh with cigarettes and age rasped in counterpoint to the music.

I was born in Kiev in 1930. I couldn't get no damn job. Not easy like it is now.

She cupped her ears, trying to block out the old man's grumbling.

We make everything for the mine. Haul timbers with a horse. No fancy equipment. We rent our house from the mines for fifty dollars a month. Only four rooms.

Rachel turned to glare at the old man sitting in a lawn chair behind her. The old man glared back. His forehead, crinkled like corduroy, was surrounded by a wisp of white hair. A belt with a silver rodeo buckle held up his pants.

This town has gone to hell. All strangers. Once I could walk down the street and say hello to ten, twenty people. Not like today. I thought I could start over.

In Centennial Park's public washroom, Rachel splashed water on her face, trying to reduce the puffiness of her eyes. Fluorescent lights hummed overhead, throwing stark shadows in the hollows by her nose. Despite the fat settling on her hips and stomach, her face was all sharp planes, discontent thickly etched from nose to mouth, as if someone had stretched the smooth skin of her twenties into a charcoal Picasso caricature. Sometimes she felt far older than thirty-two.

She left the park at midnight and walked back among crowds raving about reggae riffs. *Amazing. You could hear the Coltrane influence.* Passion. Intensity. What she'd lost.

At the campsite, her blue Nissan Sentra was gone. She'd given Jazz the spare key.

Crouching down, she unzipped the tent flap. Jazz looked up from a tangle of sleeping bags, her eyes bleary with sleep.

"Where's my car?"

"Joe took it." Jazz yawned, unconcerned.

"Did you give him the key?"

"Yeah. Vikki wanted to see the lake at the top of the mountain. They'll be back soon. Don't look so freaked. Nothing will go wrong."

Rocking back on her heels, Rachel gripped her knees to her chest, her whole body shaking. All her belongings were in the trunk of the car. She couldn't afford a new car. She had $1,600 in her bank account. She couldn't afford more problems.

Possessions that Fit in the Trunk of a Car

Two suitcases of clothes
Laptop and printer

A box of books
A box of dishes, pots and silverware

She stood up and walked away. Leaving the Wapiti campground, she came to the walking trail, a spine bisecting the town east to west. The trail paralleled the railway tracks, which smelled of creosote-soaked timbers. A train sped by, the heavy rumble of a hundred railway cars heading east. The horn blared, startlingly loud. Rachel kept walking, trying to escape her anger.

She passed several hotel parking lots full of cars, finally arriving at Railway Avenue, which turned right towards the town centre. Rachel stopped. Tears blurred her vision. The false-front buildings of Main Street faded like a bleached sepia photograph. Voices called out of the darkness. *In the old days, everyone was happier. Make your own luck. I thought I could start over.*

If only she could start over. Two summers ago, back in Canada after teaching ESL for five years in Korea, she'd met a man with silver hoops in his ears at the Vancouver Folk Festival. She'd been planning to go to grad school with the money she'd made, but it seemed like a good idea to stay in Vancouver and pick up six-month ESL teaching contracts, ignoring her lack of job security. Then her contracts ended, her rent increased, and the man walked out.

The moon was full, its glow illuminating the peaks covered with snow. Headlights flashed by, exposing her for a moment and then moving on. She turned left and crossed the overpass, stumbling occasionally in the dark, not sure where she was going. Below her, a red stream of tail lights headed for Calgary. To her left, she saw the Holiday Inn, the green *H* lit up, and behind it three hoodoos, dark spurs of rock like outthrust fingers. There was no sidewalk, so she trudged in the ditch beside the Palliser Trail. She couldn't afford a $400-a-night hotel room. She had nowhere to go. Then she saw the arched sign of the graveyard behind the Holiday Inn.

She turned down a gravel road that led to the graveyard, surrounded by a barbed wire fence. Pushing open a gate, she passed neglected graves feathered by tiny poplars. A spruce had toppled over, exposing gnarled roots. A white cross leaned crookedly against a fence. Rachel reached over and brushed her fingers against the peeling paint.

Gravestone Inscriptions
___

Anna Mather, Age Sixteen　　　　　*Viktor Prystawa*
Gone Home　　　　　　　　　　　　*Safe at Rest*

Herbert and Mabel Craig
September 26, 1918

Exhausted, her feet aching, Rachel sat down in the corner by the cross. Leaning against the fence, she listened to the shush of lodgepole pines swaying in the wind until she fell asleep, waking in the pre-dawn chill, curled on the grass, her fleece damp with dew.

The rising sun cast a red glow over the triangular peaks. Retracing her path, she left the graveyard, limping slightly. A blister rubbed on her left heel. Stones crunched under her hiking boots. She crossed the overpass, turning down Railway Avenue towards the town centre. Wandering down a street, she paused at a bridge to look down into the Bow River, dark green reeds streaming like a drowned woman's hair.

Chalets of glass and grey rock crammed the streets. Scattered between these mansions were tiny bungalows with front gardens full of old-fashioned flowers: blue bachelor's buttons, peonies, and sunflowers. On Eighth Avenue, at a white frame house with a garden full of hills of potatoes, stalks of corn, and feathery carrot tops, an old man in a fedora was picking raspberries. He came over to the fence and offered Rachel a white bowl heaped with red berries.

"Have you lived here long?" she asked, tasting a raspberry, sweetness on her lips.

All my life. Everyone else is down in the graveyard by the hoodoos, all but me. Son of a bitch, it was a good life.

"Were you happier then?"

I'm happy now. It's how you look at things. He tipped his hat.

She walked back along the road to the campground, breathing the chilly morning air. The fatty smell of bacon drifted from a propane stove where a woman in red shorts was cooking breakfast at a picnic table.

Her car was back. Rachel circled it, checking for damage. Long scrapes scored the paint on the passenger side. The front bumper on the same side was slightly crumpled, but she could drive.

Condensation fogged the windows. Peering in, Rachel saw Joe and Vikki curled up like a mismatched jigsaw puzzle, their legs awkwardly tangled.

Opening the front door, she tapped the horn twice. "Rise and shine."

Vikki pushed herself up on her elbow, peering around blindly. Her back and shoulders looked exposed against her white bra. Her fine fair hair stuck up in tangled tufts on the left side. She groped around and pulled on her tank top. Fumbled with the door handle and spilled out of the car.

Wearing only baggy jeans and socks, Joe climbed after her. He stank of alcohol. Legs shaking, he lowered himself to the grass.

"What did you hit?" Rachel asked.

"We were on a gravel road," Vikki said, "and we, like, went in the ditch. There were some bushes, I think."

Rachel reached onto the floor of the back seat, extracted a pair of pink flip-flops, and dumped Joe's knapsack on the road. Unlacing her hiking boots, she pulled off her socks, wrinkling her nose at the stale smell, and slipped on her sandals.

"I want my key back." Standing over him, she held out her right hand. Joe looked up at her, his eyes narrowed. Then he pulled the key from his pocket and dropped it into her hand.

Jazz had crawled out of the tent, wrapped in a red-checked sleeping bag. She had the anxious yet anticipatory look of someone watching a couple fight, unsure whether to step in or let the whole thing blow over.

Rachel climbed into the driver's seat, started the car, and then rolled down the window. "I'm leaving. Find your own ride back."

"Wait a sec." Jazz hobbled over, barefoot, wincing at the sharpness of the gravel. "What's your problem? He brought it back. No big deal."

"Do you see the scrapes on the passenger side?"

"So we'll pay you for damages."

"Right," Rachel said flatly.

Jazz hesitated and then shrugged. "Whatever. We'll get home somehow."

Rachel sprayed gravel pulling out of the campsite. At the Trans-Canada, she turned west, cranking the radio — k.d. lang singing "Constant Craving." Once, she'd been an anticipation junkie. Anything could happen. Now the thought was terrifying.

Near the Crowsnest Pass, she heard a hideous squealing noise, like a pig being killed. Rachel pulled onto the shoulder and pounded the steering wheel several times.

"What the fuck!"

She got out and checked under the hood. Everything looked normal. She tried driving forward on the shoulders and the hideous squealing started again. What did she know about cars? Nothing. She had an AMA membership her dad had bought her, saying, "Better safe than sorry." Maybe it was still good.

A hot wind whipped her hair as she stood on the shoulder, wondering what she would do next. An hour later the tow truck arrived. The sandy-haired AMA mechanic took off the front tire on the passenger side. "Here's your problem. There's a rock between the brake pad and the dust shield. You got lucky this time."

Aphorisms

> *Whatever*
> *It's how you look at things*
> *You got lucky this time*

Rachel drove west.

Searching for Spock

THE YEAR KALLA WAS TWELVE, her grandma walked out the front door and didn't come back.

"What could I do?" Kalla overheard her mother say a few days later. Kalla was lying on the living room sofa, reading *Little Women*. Her mother was on the phone. "I told him he couldn't bring her here. But he showed up at the front door. I couldn't turn them away."

She was speaking about Kalla's grandfather and his new girlfriend. *Girlfriend*. The word was somehow wrong for this heavyset woman in her fifties, with short dark hair and hand-sewn peasant smocks. Her sixty-five-year-old grandfather, with his white beard and long white hair brushing his shoulder, seemed far too old to have a girlfriend. He smelled of peppermints, mothballs and wool, and walked with a slight limp, the after-effects of a car accident he'd suffered three years earlier when his pelvis was shattered after another driver ran a red light and T-boned his car.

Her grandma had lived with them after the separation, sleeping downstairs in what had been the TV room. Kalla and her sister shared a bedroom upstairs, their canopy beds with the flowery purple and light blue bedspreads filling the square space.

Every morning at five, she heard her grandmother climb the stairs and light up the first cigarette of the day. Then she would start baking: cinnamon buns with raisins and icing, loaves of bread, ginger cookies, deep-fried donuts. By six, the kitchen smelled of crystallized brown sugar and yeast with a bitter overlay of smoke. Pans of baking covered the stove, and her grandmother would be soaking dirty dishes in a sink full of sudsy water. In six months, Kalla gained fifteen pounds on her five-foot-two frame, transforming from a slim child to a pudgy adolescent.

Her grandma never ate any of the baking. She was short but weighed only ninety-eight pounds. Her thick knuckles were twisted by arthritis, the fingernails stained yellow by cigarettes. She had several irregular dark moles on her cheeks and forehead. When she was young, her hair had been strawberry blonde, like Kalla's, but she suffered a bout of scarlet fever in her early twenties and her hair fell out. It grew back a grizzled dark brown.

One day while Kalla was combing her hair, her grandma came into the bathroom and stood beside her. They were the same height, had the same colouring, except Kalla's eyes were pale blue rather than hazel.

"Look at my skin," her grandma said. Kalla looked at the triangle of black moles on her grandmother's left cheek, the deep lines stretching from the corner of the nose to the mouth, the grey pouches beneath her grandmother's hazel eyes. Then she looked at her own peachy complexion, with a smatter of freckles across the nose.

"Look after your skin," her grandma said. "I had skin like you once. Don't go out in the sun. Wear a hat. Use sunscreen.

You don't want to end up looking like me." It sounded like a curse.

Kalla was in a new school, one of those low single-story elementary schools built for the influx of children who came to Alberta for the oil boom. In her sixth-grade class, Kalla was surrounded by a Karen, a Callee, a Kendra. She made the mistake of telling these girls that her mother had named her for a flower, a Calla lily.

"You don't look like a flower," Callee said. She was the head of the popular clique, a tall skinny girl with dark hair. Sometimes when the teachers called Kalla's name, Callee would answer. Her name wasn't pronounced Caylee, like an Irish party, but Call-ee, like California. She said, "Unless it's a stinkweed. Who gives their kid a stupid name like stinkweed?"

After that moment, the girls in the clique — Callee, Kendra, Lori, and Karen — called Kalla "stinkweed," along with the other names: fat, stupid, ugly.

Kalla spent her teen years in a dark basement, watching *Buffy the Vampire Slayer*, *FireFly*, and reruns of *Star Trek* on the Space channel, and reading comics: *X-Men*, *Watchmen*, *Elfquest*. Comics about people who were different, but special. Nightcrawler, who could transport from one place to another. Storm, who could harness the elements. She read about superheroes punishing evil and protecting the innocent, and she imagined all the vengeance she would inflict on the girls in the popular clique, Callee and Lori and Karen, who had migrated with her to Scona High School.

She also spent most of her teen years on diets, trying to lose those fifteen pounds she'd gained. She cut out bread, sugar, cookies, white rice. She cut out nearly all the foods she liked and lived on lean protein, brown rice, vegetables, and fruit for four years.

When she was seventeen, Kalla shortened her name to Kal, an androgynous name. She dyed her hair copper red and wore black jeans and black T-shirts with skull motifs. She told friends in university that she had been named for Kali, the Hindu goddess of death, the black goddess with her necklace of skulls.

Her grandmother remained missing. Kalla stopped asking her parents if her grandmother would return. As far as she could tell, her father made no effort to find his mother. Like Spock in *Star Trek*, her father kept his emotions hidden. Spock: half Vulcan, half human, controlled by logic. In Spock, Kal felt her own split personality: logic and emotion.

When Kalla graduated with an MA in English, the recession was gutting education in Alberta, and she worked for a year as a substitute teacher. Now she had a one-year contract at Mount Royal College, teaching two first-year English classes. She could teach *The Chrysalids, Ender's Game, Animal Farm, The Hobbit,* even graphic novels like *Sandman* and *The Watchmen*. Heroes and villains.

In February, she had assigned her students a creative short story. "Make it real," she told them. For many of them that meant writing about their own lives. Stories about bullying. Stories about breakups. Stories about death. Her students pared back the flesh to reveal the heart.

Serena, a tiny black-haired girl, who wore bright red lipstick and equally bright fuchsia tops, had written an explicit account of bullying.

Serena's classmates called her a skank and a loser. They spread rumours about her, snapped her bra strap during gym class, called her ugly. Serena couldn't take the bullying anymore. She pulled out a steak knife and slashed her wrist.

In class, Serena was overly vivacious, her hand shooting up to answer questions. But now, early April, she had been absent for a month. She'd failed every grammar quiz. Her 800-word essay on *Animal Farm* was a month late.

As a teacher, Kal vowed she would never embarrass or single out a student. Her own ethical code. She recalled a class in her second year of university, when the English 356 professor sneered, "You seem to be in the wrong class," as he handed back her paper. Looking at the front page, she realized she'd transposed two numbers: the class number read English 365, a simple typo. On the back page was a scrawled C-. No comments. The clues that he was a jerk had been there the first day, when he said "That's a bullet dodged" after an Asian student peeked in the door, asked if this was the room for History 101, and then left.

Of course, she had singled out students this year. When they pulled out forbidden cell phones, when they spent the entire class whispering and giggling, when they quickly pulled down laptop screens so she wouldn't see that they were playing *Call of Duty*, she put on her teacher face to maintain discipline. Students had their own world with clear social hierarchies. Teachers were outsiders.

Sometimes, like her grandmother, she wanted to run away. Faced with a desk piled high with student papers, a sink full of dishes, and a dwindling bank account, she imagined dropping everything and walking out of her life. But she didn't know where she would go.

She went to Comic Con at the Calgary Agricom. The line of costumed adults stretched from the door of the main hall to the stairs of the C-train platform. For twenty minutes, the line didn't move. A chilly April breeze blew. Kal shivered in her fleece pullover.

A girl with jet-black asymmetrical hair, like a twenties flapper, complained, "This is bullshit. I bought my ticket months ago. Why isn't the line moving?" Below a bright yellow miniskirt, her bare legs pimpled with goose bumps.

Nightcrawler turned around. "They're oversold. There's no room in the main hall." His long blue tail, wired to stand in a half-U, swished through the flap of a long black coat.

"I've never been to one of these before," Kal said. "I read that Spock is here."

"He must be in his seventies. Hard to believe."

"Forty years since the original *Star Trek*." She'd grown up watching reruns of the original series on *Space*. She needed to establish her nerd cred since she wasn't in costume. She had on jeans and a black T-shirt printed with a Day of the Dead sugar skull, blue flowers decorating the eye sockets. Her own version of a uniform.

Spock was the draw. Leonard Nimoy, coming from a conference in Vulcan, Alberta, had just announced his retirement. Last chance to see Spock.

The line surged forward as the doors opened into a concrete warehouse crammed with aliens, vampires, middle-aged men in Star Trek uniforms, busty girls in medieval dresses with flowers in their hair. All the freaks, geeks, Goths, nerds, Trekkies, cosplayers, all the kids who never fit in, all together.

Pushing through the clot by the front doors, Kal moved through the masses. Her grandma, a British citizen raised in India, had taught her a trick for dealing with crowds. "Think of the people as statues," she'd say. Kal slid past Batman posing for pictures, zigged past Queen Amidala in harem pants and a bikini top, and zagged to avoid a clump of teens with *anime* haircuts.

Now she was in the far corner of the warehouse, near the food stands selling perogies, mini-donuts, and hot dogs. She bought a large latte to fortify herself for the line for Spock's autograph. An autograph alone cost $20. If she wanted a picture with him, it would be $100.

The lineup to see Spock already stretched the length of the main hall, curving past closed doors to workshops with lesser celebrities (writers, illustrators, directors), reaching into the warehouse divided into aisles crowded with comic book stalls and T-shirt vendors. Kal joined the line behind a large woman with a prominent bald spot in her thinning black hair. Sipping her latte, she settled in for a long wait.

A weedy kid wandered by in thick platform boots, a brocade tan waistcoat and jeans, an eighteenth-century lord. He was holding the hand of a steampunk girl in a tightly laced crimson bustier, black tulle and lace foaming over a short black skirt, ribbed tights worn with thigh-high black boots. Where did they get their costumes? Geek had never looked so chic when Kal was in university.

After reading Serena's story of slashing her wrists, she had called Serena in during office hours for a talk. "I'm concerned about your story. The cutting seems quite serious."

"Please don't report me. Please." Serena started crying. "It was in high school. I'm okay now. Please don't report me."

Kal handed her a tissue, waited for her to stop weeping.

"I'm not going to report you." Kal promised. "I just wanted you to know about the counselling services the school has. I was worried about you."

Serena kept repeating, "Please don't report me."

Serena's reaction seemed extreme. She hadn't been back to class since the talk. Maybe she felt she couldn't slip back into the herd now.

Would she report a fantasy about bringing a gun to school? Yes. But a story about bullying and cutting was less clear. The department guidelines were not helpful: *Remember that communication is the key! Trust your intuition and report your concerns.* She didn't report the story until Serena had missed a month of class.

"So why are you reporting the story now?" the head of her department asked. Kal felt the floor slip beneath her. A sudden sinking in her stomach. This was how her students felt, sitting on the other side of a desk, across from someone who held all the power. The department head was a tall woman in a bright red tunic dress and dark-framed glasses. She was saying, *Why are you getting me involved?* And even worse: *Why can't you handle this on your own?*

The department head told her to contact Student Services. "The number is in the Instructor Guidelines," she said, making the process seem obvious. Kal left the office feeling that she had screwed any chances of another job. Her contract was renewable, but only if the college was satisfied with her work.

Kal had been waiting in line for an hour and fifteen minutes when the latte kicked in. She needed to pee. Right now. The line snaked past the washrooms. Kal looked ahead. There were at least 100 people in front of her.

"Excuse me," she said to the woman in front of her in line. "I just need to duck out of the line for a moment and use the washroom. Would you mind holding my spot?"

"Actually, I would."

"I'm sorry?" Was this woman, this Trekkie, refusing such a simple request? Like Kal, the woman was in ordinary clothes, black leggings and a green smock top covering wide hips.

"You can go to the back of the line if you need to leave."

"That would mean another hour in line. I've already waited over an hour."

"If you're not willing to wait, I guess you're not a real fan."

Kal left the line. When had the world become so angry? If a person who claimed to be a *Star Trek* fan, a Spock fan, could be such a bitch, was there any hope for understanding?

Her last chance to see Spock was gone. He would never return to Canada.

Kal waited until she was in a washroom stall before she started crying. She knew about bullies. Her family had moved from Vancouver to Edmonton when Kal was in grade six. The first month she was walking home from school, past a small park rimmed with dark spruce trees in the centre of a cul-de-sac of bungalows. Three boys about her age were kicking around a soccer ball in a grassy area by the sidewalk.

As Kal walked by, one of them picked up a stone and threw it, just missing her head. Kal turned around, shocked, and the next stone grazed her, gashing a line down her forearm. She ran, stones pelting around her, hitting her back and calves. After that she walked along the main road to school, avoiding the shortcut.

She had no friends that year. During recess, Callee and the group of popular girls would chant, "Kalla lily, Kalla lily, she is fat and ugly." And there were other names. Her mother told her, "Sticks and stones may break my bones, but words will never hurt me." The stones hurt where they grazed her arm and legs. The words hurt more.

After splashing water on her face to reduce the puffiness around her eyes and remove the smeared mascara, she walked down the long hallway, past the booths selling comic books, signed *anime* posters, and movie memorabilia, and pushed open the double doors. Outside, snow swirled around the Agricom.

In March, a social worker at a care home had called her parents. Her grandma had had a small stroke and had been in hospital overnight, but she was back in the room she'd lived in for ten years. The social worker said she'd asked what relatives to contact, and Mrs. Martin had given her the phone number.

Kal's father refused to go the first time. Kal's mother drove down and picked up Kal in Calgary and then drove them both to Lethbridge, but she too refused to go into the care home. Maybe she was afraid that her mother-in-law would slam the door in her face. The force of will in that tiny person — fourteen years of silence and absence to make a point about betrayal.

At the door of the room, Kal hesitated and then knocked. She'd wondered if she would recognize her grandma, but she looked just the same, a tiny woman with frizzled grey hair, her wrinkled skin a darker shade than ivory. An orange sweater dwarfed her tiny frame.

"Grandma," Kal said.

"Kalla. You finally came," her grandma said, as if she had left clues and Kal had been negligent in finding them or she had just left a few days ago. She pulled Kal into the single room, which had a sofa piled high with balls of wool, a single bed, a table and two chairs tucked into a corner by the tiny kitchen.

"I walked out on that man," her grandma whispered to her, as if she had been waiting all those years to tell someone. "He wasn't a nice person. He left me for another woman." Years of grievances spilled out.

Kal's favourite Spock scene was at the end of *Star Trek: The Wrath of Khan*. *The Enterprise* is badly damaged, the hyperdrive non-functioning. Shields are failing. Spock goes down to the engine room, disables Dr. McCoy with a Vulcan nerve pinch, enters the engine room filled with radiation and repairs the engine. Dying, Spock says to Kirk, *The needs of the many outweigh the needs of the few. Or the one.* His Kobayashi Maru, an unwinnable scenario

She had failed her own Kobayashi Maru. She had betrayed a student, broken her word.

She hadn't heard anything back from Serena or Student Services since contacting them. A long silence. Silence has its own power.

The Apostles

*A*FTER THEIR DEATHS, I WANTED *to run to the end of the earth. I wanted to step off the edge of the world, to descend into black waters. I went to a place where the centre is rock, red as blood, and the ocean surrounds you on all sides.*

Paul stood on the shore of the lake, looking over its luminous black ripples. He had not been back in two years. Walking down the stretch of sand, he discarded his clothing at the water's edge. The ground fell away beneath his feet.

He swam into the lake, ten lengths, twenty. He swam away from the past, but it followed him, music rising off the surface of the water like evening mist. Simon and Garfunkel, their voices twining together in the ballad "Cecilia."

He knew before he saw her that she was in the water. Her hair, slicked down by the water, was as glossy as a seal's pelt.

"They're here," she said. "I can feel them, hovering above your head. Aren't you afraid to come back? Peter was."

Peter, who in this spot he could hear clearly, whose voice called out of the broken past.

When my visa expired, I stayed on in Australia. There are guys there, American 'Nam vets, with no visas. A colony lives up in the mountains outside Cairns. I took a train, snaking over canyons, passing over an abyss of time. The sixties are still happening there. They're up in the mountains, selling tarnished silver and tie-dyed dreams.

The moon rose, a glowing crescent in the eastern sky. Light fell in sheets, reflected from the darkness of Cecilia's eyes.

They had come to the cabin that Peter's parents owned but never used. Left unlocked, the cabin remained untouched by vandals or time: four small rooms, the walls permeated by the smoky haze of memories.

Sitting before the fire, they tried to bridge the gap between past and present time. She would say, *Do you remember when?* and he would match the pieces of her puzzle. But it remained as broken as the beer bottles they had thrown against stop signs. Time blurred into broken shards and he was alone with Cecilia, sitting in faded armchairs before the stone fireplace. Two old friends, reminiscing, while voices and visions swirled around the room.

Sitting in darkness, with only the red flicker of flames to cast an aureole around Cecilia's cap of dark hair, Paul saw the ghosts rising from the walls and taking shape before him. Peter, with flames shining through him and turning the bottle of rye in his hands to gold. Even in the flesh, Peter had seemed insubstantial, subject to moments of disappearance. Cecilia once said, "Peter is a shadow; he needs to stand behind someone." And so, after the accident, Peter began to fade, like a photograph left too long in the acid bath. Behind Peter's skeletal form, Paul could see the wall of fire and jagged rock. Peter raised the bottle of rye to his lips and drank. A golden line trailed down the inside of his throat, then bubbled up again in words, harsh as a crow's caw.

Near the equator, the dividing line, the sun sets every night at six, a flash of orange and red and it's gone, falling into the line of the ocean. Stars shine in all the wrong places. A cross hangs in the sky. The dipper vanished and I couldn't follow its handle down to the North Star. The nights are darker when the moon shines silver on unfamiliar waters and even the stars are strangers. I had to leave, turn tail and run south.

Paul saw a flash of light from the other side of the fireplace. The glow blinded him. Bright spots danced before his closed eyelids. A whiff of rose petals. He opened his eyes to blackness.

The past was a wave of dark water rushing towards him. Down and down he fell, the past overwhelming him: down past summer days of sun and laughter; down past evenings of music as they strummed their guitars, smoking bitter grass; down past nights when he and Cecilia tumbled together, like the balls of green and gold that Marina juggled in the daylight hours. Marina, her waterfall of shining hair falling to her knees, her smile as bright as a sunflower as she turned towards Jay. Marina laughing in the sun, while Peter basked in his brother's shadow.

Marina and Jay splashed by the dock, Marina floating on the water, her skin white in the July sun. Paul stood watching on the platform anchored out in the lake while Cecilia and Peter swam towards him, light shining off their brown arms, off the foaming wave kicked up by their legs, Cecilia reaching him first, grabbing his ankle and down he fell, into deep waters, over his head, choking, water in his mouth, his nose, water blinding his eyes, and then the slippery chill of Cecilia's limbs against his, her hand in his, pulling him up, out of the water, out of the past, rising through layers of memory back into this moment.

I fled south, from Cairns to Sydney, snaking down the coast, past endless ghost trees and dead kangas by the side of the road, past the Gold Coast where the money-makers roast their bodies brown as shit, their smiles white and deadly as the sharks' teeth they wear around their necks. I came to a city with buildings like sails and miles and miles of sand, glittering like glass. I washed my feet in the fountain at King's Cross where prostitutes showed their wares.

They slept that night coupled like spoons, her back curved into his chest, his chin resting on the line of her neck. Her hair, still wet from the midnight swim, dripped against his cheek. He dreamt he floated in an immense blue lake of grinning sharks and grey trees with ghostly arms. Cecilia swam up to him, her eyes as large as saucers. "Aren't you afraid?" she asked. He stood in a garden of roses on the sandy floor and saw Marina by a rosebush, her loose hair crowned by a bridal wreath of crimson buds. Sunlight, falling through the water, struck her hair and turned it to fire. She held her hands out to him: red roses dripped from her fingers. "What are you doing here?" The words rose through the water in brightly coloured bubbles: green, blue, and gold. "I am tending his grave."

He woke to sunlight on his face. The soft murmur of voices rose from the kitchen. Someone said something, and he heard the chime of Marina's laughter falling in perfect thirds, and then Jay's voice joined in, a deep bass, warm and soothing as liquid honey. He struggled against the weight of the sleeping bag, trying to get up

And woke in the small room in the pre-dawn quiet. Dust motes hung in the air. Beside him, Cecilia curled up in a ball, her head protected under her left arm.

Paul slipped out of bed, out of the cottage. A mist was rising from the lake. He followed the path to the shore.

Peter waited for him on the sand.

In Australia, I was surrounded by water. The cities perch on the edge of nothing, cling to tide-swept beaches. I met this guy, another damned war vet, in a hostel in Sydney. We were going to drive to the centre, the heart of Australia. The rock. Uluru. But first he wanted to see this natural miracle, these pillars in the ocean. The apostles.

After breakfast, they took the rowboat out. Cecilia wore a white robe over her swimsuit.

Paul rowed slowly, staying close to the east shore. He passed the dock, the swimming platform. Behind him, over his left shoulder, were the two tiny islands.

Out on the water, there was only a thick silence.

They passed the first island, moved into the channel formed between the two. Here, the water was shallow: sharp rocks scraped against his oars.

"Just past the island," Cecilia said. "They found the boat just past the islands."

Paul rowed four more strokes, then stopped, shipped the oars.

Cecilia put on flippers, dipped her mask in water, and then fastened it. While Paul steadied the boat, she slipped over the side.

"Hand me the flashlight," she said. Her voice muffled, as if she was already speaking from underwater. A quick splash, a flash of red bathing suit, then flippers, and she was gone.

He was alone in the small boat, on the blue of a lake studded with islands. This close to the spot, Peter was silenced. But over the flat surface of the water, skipping like light or a flat stone, came Marina's voice. No words, none that he could understand. It could have been a Gaelic lament. To him, it was a wash of long vowels, as plaintive as the soft rain falling on the roof of the room where he and Cecilia slept. So many nights they had fallen asleep together while Marina's liquid vowels tumbled above the chords of Jay's guitar. They would sleep in one of the back rooms while Peter slept in the other, and Marina and Jay sang and played through the night.

Cecilia rose to the surface, sputtering. "Damn mask." Water sloshed against her cheeks above the seal. She pulled it off, disappeared again beneath the water

This time he could understand the words to the music. Cat Stevens, one of Jay's favourite singers. A lament for a loved one. The music transposed into a higher key so that Marina's voice, as pure as an Anglican choirboy's unbroken soprano, soared into the blue cathedral of sky.

The song ended. Silence. The sun shone. Time dragged. Paul checked his watch. Cecilia had been underwater for close to four minutes.

Looking over the side, he searched for the spot of light that would show her presence. The water was black in the shadow of the boat, green a little further off, white where the sunlight glared off it.

Cecilia surfaced a few feet away. For a moment, she floated in the water, gasping for breath or weeping. Her hair clung to her head like a shiny black cap. She swam over, hooked her arms over the boat's side. Paul pulled her in.

"Nothing. Only the circle of my flashlight. And grey rocks."

From the towel at her feet, she took out a dried rose, its petals red as crusted blood. Around its stem, she wrapped a silver chain with a small cross. "It was Marina's," she said.

Cecilia dropped the rose on the water. It rested for a moment, and then the anchor of the cross pulled it down and it sank. Paul grasped the oars and turned the boat around.

Peter's voice drifted out to meet them as Paul rowed the last few strokes back to the dock.

The apostles. There are twelve of them, these giant pillars of rock. They were part of the mainland until the waves got them. The waves eat in every year, crumbling rock, mining the edges of the cliffs. Busloads of tourists come and take pictures. That's what the 'Nam vet was pretending to be — some dumb tourist. He even had a broken camera slung around his neck. There are signs posted: STAND BACK FROM THE EDGE. Crazy, but you know what I thought? I thought of the signs I'd seen in the city. No standing. It means no parking. I walked out to the edge of the cliff and stood there.

That night they fried hamburgers on the stone barbecue built into the patio. Paul found some dry wood under the cottage eaves and burnt it down to coals. They drank red wine as the sun set, and then went back into the main room and lit a fire. And they tried again to put together the pieces.

The last night of summer, the end of the hiatus, the end of dreaming. Their shadowy forms emerged: Paul in one chair with Cecilia on his lap; Marina in the other with Jay at her feet; Peter sitting on the hearth. A bottle of rye passed around the circle and a joint. It had been raining all day and they had a fire burning. The light cast half of their faces in shadow, like Egyptian hieroglyphics. They talked and talked. Marina always talked with her hands, and he could see the patterns her white fingers traced through the air. At one point, Cecilia brought in crackers and cheese and brownies. Then they brought out their guitars, Cecilia played her flute, and Peter drummed time against his knee.

And there the memory ended. Paul could see them grouped around the fire, Cecilia now standing, Jay and Marina cradling their guitars. But what happened for the next hours, what they played and sang and said and dreamed was gone. The next clear picture was the back room where he and Cecilia slept, cradled together. He had jerked awake to the panic of Peter's sobbing, the frantic words "the boat, the boat" repeated over and over, a scratch on a record, the needle catching over and over. Then he heard Peter's voice.

I'm standing there on the edge of the cliff and I hear them screaming, "Get back here, you stupid bugger, you asshole," and I keep standing there, waiting for the ground to crumble. I tried to walk out into the air, but my feet were fastened to the cliff. I perched there like a bird, clinging to the edge. And I knew. Even if

I moved, the air would hold me up. There would be no falling into immortality for me.

They left the cabin the next morning. In the city, they met each Wednesday at a downtown restaurant, sitting on a rooftop terrace while the traffic snarled below them. Cecilia drank red wine and the light glowed through it, staining the white enamelled table.

In the city, Paul could barely hear Peter's voice. He saw the Australian desert and its central rock, blood-red in the early sunrise; he heard the panting breath of the pilgrims as they climbed. Cecilia was wearing a T-shirt on which a tiny stick figure on a red boulder shouted: I climbed Ayers Rock.

"He sent it to me," Cecilia said. "He sent it to me the day before he climbed the rock."

He showed her the last postcard. The picture on the front was long cylindrical pillars, like the hoodoos of the Alberta badlands. An impossibly blue ocean lapped at the rocks, feathering the bases with whitecaps. Diagonal printing across the front of the card read: The Twelve Apostles. On the other side was Peter's message. *Water, water everywhere. Australia is surrounded by water. Even at the rock.*

Paul looked over the edge and saw the long fall to the red sand.

They sat on the terrace, under the shade of a striped umbrella. Waiters in neon boxer shorts, patterned with black fish and palm trees, topped with white tank tops, wove by them with trays of drinks held high. The light fell around them in bright sheets, blinding their vision.

Cutting Edge

" RIGHT, IT'S AGREED. FRIDAY, WE infiltrate *Cutting Edge* and take back our work."

Harry had joined the writing circle after reading a notice in the weekly free paper, *Look*, calling for local writers to share their work in a nonjudgmental format. Their hangout was the Red Dog, a Whyte Avenue bar with beer-stained oak floors and a high black ceiling. At the first meeting, Harry read his latest song lyric, about a truck driver from Beaver Lodge who experiments with mushrooms and pines for a stripper.

"Awesome. You should send that to *The Fern*," said Rob, a weedy man in baggy jeans and a T-shirt with the Statue of Liberty holding a gun. Anarchist chic, from his matted blond dreads to his mud-stained Doc Martens. He'd had work read on CJSR and two years ago *The Fern* had sent him an encouraging rejection letter.

"Don't send it there." K'lyn, the only woman in the group, had established her credentials immediately by reading one of her published poems. "The editor's an alcoholic; he only takes stories about Guinness and bars. Why don't you send it to *Cutting Edge*? It's a local journal. Hell, we should all send something. We're local writers. I wonder what they pay."

Harry sent his lyrics, disguised as poetry with some odd line breaks. Rob sent a twenty- page story about a one-legged cocaine addict who burns down a newspaper office. K'lyn submitted nine poems about breakups, complete with creative ideas for dismembering old boyfriends. They sat back and waited. Five months later, they were still waiting. Rob fired off some emails, and then called an emergency meeting.

"This is bullshit," he said. "They won't even reply to my emails. What kind of journal are they running?"

The plan was simple. Rob was a member of an anarchist group that had ties to the local Small Press Association, which shared an office in the downtown public library with *Cutting Edge*. Rob had gone to the monthly meeting of the Small Press Association and palmed a key.

"We'll break into the office on Friday night. No one has meetings on Friday."

Harry said, "I have a gig on Friday." He played fiddle for a Celtic group. Maybe K'lyn would show up. After all, it was Celtic music and she was from Saint John. K'lyn had rippling red hair, pale skin dotted with clots of freckles, bright blue eyes. A classic recessive, created out of generations of Scots, Irish, and Acadians interbreeding with impunity, she was just what Harry imagined an Irish lass should look like, with a temper to match the red hair. He could impress her with his solo in McGinty's Reel. Harry tried not to think about the fishing net draped in front of the stage at the Trap and Swill to deflect the beer bottles that drunks threw when the band didn't play *Great Big Sea* covers.

"So we'll go early."

"I work until nine on Friday." Drew worked at Staples. Each meeting, he'd read one of his bitter vignettes about work at an unnamed retail outlet, full of repetitive dialogue from a couple of Neanderthals, and then get shit-faced on a pitcher of beer.

"Look, we don't all have to be there," Rob said. "I think Harry, K'lyn, and I can manage."

Harry glowed with pride. Rob preferred his help to Drew's. At three hundred pounds, Harry was usually discounted from any physical activity. "So when's the hit?" He felt like a member of Al Capone's gang. He saw himself with his violin case loaded with a Tommy gun, blasting his way through the library. Redistributing those fat cat government grants. Getting some for the little guy.

That night, he told his landlord about the planned heist. Marc, a functioning drunk who repaired musical instruments, had called him up to sample a twenty-five-year-old Scotch.

"Sweet talk yer throat and burn yer arse it will!" Marc promised.

Pulling over an old chrome kitchenette chair, Harry settled his girth, the chair legs bowing under the strain. He placed his bag of MacBaren Danish Burley amid the remains of a dismantled accordion and pulled his favourite Meerschaum from the inner pocket of his fleece. Marc, unlike the anti-smoking fascists at City Hall, encouraged indoor smoking.

After they'd debated the merits of single malt, Harry lamented the state of Canadian publishing.

"No one appreciates good writing. It's all part of the dumbing down of society. Like that shithole of a Christian school in Grande Prairie. They didn't teach; they just shoved Bible lessons down our throats. I didn't read *Hamlet* until university. Plus, they beat the crap out of us any chance they got."

"Just like bloody England," Marc agreed. "My headmaster treated us like conscripts, tried to beat some sense into us. He'd been a commando in the marines, you see. Not that it didn't do us good. I can still remember some of the poetry he spouted."

Harry listened to Marc recite Tennyson's *The Kraken* from memory, awed by this grasp of the great works of English literature. He'd been born fifty years and twelve hundred miles from where his soul truly belonged. No wonder he couldn't get any work published here. His work was too deep. Editors, like magpies, were attracted by the simple and shiny.

"Oh, and you'll be owing me this month's rent," Marc said. "Just leave the money on the table, there's a good lad."

Harry pulled out his wallet. Four lonely twenties stared back at him.

"I'm a bit short this month, Marc."

"Are you now? If you wouldn't be splurging on that fancy tobacco, you might have the money. Well, pay me what you can now."

Harry pulled out the eighty dollars, woefully aware that it was less than a quarter of what he owed. "I'll get you the rest on Friday, after my gig," he promised. Well, he would have some of the money, if he remembered not to drink during sets. The last time the band played there, they'd ended up owing the bar money for the tab. It would be KD and tuna for the rest of the month.

On Friday, he took a bus to the downtown library, threaded past the panhandlers guarding the front door, and waited twenty minutes in the reading area on the main floor, where old men slumped wearily on black couches, waiting to be thrown out into the night.

K'lyn and Rob arrived together at seven-thirty. K'lyn insisted on browsing the poetry stacks before they went upstairs, so they would seem like regular library patrons.

They hit a snafu at the elevators. The office was on the sixth floor. Rob pushed the button. The doors closed, and then opened again.

"What the fuck?" Rob went over the check-out desk. Harry and K'lyn loitered by the elevators, trying to look inconspicuous.

Rob came back with a bullet-headed tattooed security guard in his fifties.

"I didn't hear about any meetings tonight." He glared at them. "You're supposed to book meetings a day in advance."

"We just have to pick up a few papers." K'lyn turned on him with a wide-toothed smile.

"Well, I don't know, little lady. What organization is it again?"

"*Cutting Edge*. We're on the poetry collective," she lied coolly. "We have to pick up a batch of submissions."

"Well, if you're quick about it." Pulling a thick key ring from his belt, he slowly sorted through them, making them wait. Inserting a key into the electronic panel, he twisted it, and then pressed the sixth-floor button.

"Thank you so much," K'lyn gushed. As the elevator doors closed, her smile blinked out. "Could you believe that? Little lady. What a sexist pig."

On the sixth floor, Rob lingered by the elevators in case the guard decided to follow them. Harry and K'lyn walked past a line of doors to the end of the hall. At the door to the *Cutting*

Edge office, Harry inserted the key and slowly twisted it in the lock. It stuck.

"Hurry the fuck up," whispered K'lyn.

He twisted the key harder. The key bent. Harry let go. "Shit. I think I've broken it."

"Ahh, get the fuck out of the way." Pushing her way past his bulk, K'lyn jiggled the key back and forth, muttering "Damn it, damn it" under her breath. She twisted too vigorously, and the key snapped in her hand. "Christ! What the fuck did you do to it, Harry?"

"I just turned it."

Rob came down the hall. "Aren't you guys in yet? The guard will be checking on us any minute. How hard is it to open a door?"

"Harry broke the key."

Harry started to protest, and then realized this wouldn't help him in K'lyn's eyes. Instead, he held up his hands, palms outstretched in apology.

"Great, just great," said Rob. "It cost me five bucks to copy that damned key."

The elevator pinged its arrival.

"The guard's coming." Harry looked frantically down the long bare hall. No place to hide. He saw them, like rats in a maze, going endlessly round and round the corridors, the guard always one step behind. He started wheezing with anxiety.

Rob pounded the door in frustration. It swung open. They spilled into the room.

Long tubes of fluorescent lighting flickered slowly to life. Partitions divided the room into three sections. Rob led them to the back corner where *Cutting Edge* had its office. Bookcases lined two walls, sagging under the weight of past issues. Brown eight-by-eleven envelopes were stacked around the edges of the computer monitor, obscuring the printer.

"Christ, do they ever answer their mail?" K'lyn shuffled through a stack, pulled out an envelope at random and opened it. "Look at this cover letter. May 2005. That's over a year ago and they haven't even opened it."

"Look at their computer," Harry said in awe. "A heavily modded, fully loaded Dell XPS 700 in fire-engine red. That's a three-thousand-dollar machine. And they have a multifunction HP LaserJet 4345. And a flat screen."

K'lyn nodded sagely. "Canada Council grants. Someone must be a gamer."

"What if we take some old issues and sell them?" Harry wondered. "They wouldn't miss them."

"Don't be so stupid," K'lyn laughed. "Old issues won't sell."

"We said we're taking the submissions." Rob took charge. "Let's take them all. Then we'll leave ours and a few of the really crappy ones. They'll have to publish our stuff."

"Awesome idea." K'lyn beamed on Rob, like a teacher with a prize pupil. Harry sulked.

They stuffed envelopes into K'lyn's Guatemalan book bag. Harry dug a plastic Safeway bag out of the garbage for the remainder.

"What if the writers ask about their stuff?" he asked.

"We'll have to send them rejection letters. Hack into the computer and find the form."

While he was searching, K'lyn and Rob read over some of the submissions.

"Listen to this," K'lyn giggled. *"Dear Sir, I am sending you some of my immortal prose. I have been writing for several years now, but just began sending it out this year.* We're definitely leaving this one in. How not to write a submission letter."

"Here's the form." Harry looked over to where K'lyn and Rob sat on a tweedy orange couch. The sleeve of K'lyn's filmy red blouse brushed against Rob's arm. Both of them turned their heads at the same angle. Synchronization. Harry had watched a nature show on the mating habits of birds, how they mimicked each other's moves. Here it was, right under his nose.

"Just print up some copies. We'll fill in the names later."

"How many?"

"Christ, Harry, make a decision on your own for once." K'lyn stroked Rob's arm. "Here's another great one. *Love / a busy bee / sipping nectar from my heart.* That's gotta hurt."

As the final copies of the letter spat out of the printer, Harry thought of something else. "What about the key in the door? If the envelopes are missing, they'll ask questions."

"Damn. And the guard will remember us. A redhead, a guy in a Che Guevara T-shirt, and a fat man with a violin. Sounds like a fucking joke." K'lyn looked to Rob for answers. "What do you think we should do?"

"We'll sort these at the Red Dog tonight," Rob said. "I'll bring the rejects in tomorrow morning. They won't be meeting on the weekend. As long as the guard doesn't notice the door is broken, we'll be fine."

"I can't go. I have the gig." His visions of the way the evening would play out had evaporated. The signs were clear. Thin anarchist trumps fat musician.

He pulled open several drawers, looking for envelopes. In the top left-hand drawer was an envelope with the words "Float" written on it. Harry gave it a surreptitious shake. Coins jingled.

Checking over his shoulder, Harry saw that K'lyn and Rob had moved to the next step of the mating dance. He casually slid his hand into the float, extracted some loonies.

"Hey, can you guys give me a ride to the A&W?" He'd feast on a double burger combo before the gig, courtesy of *Cutting Edge*. If he was sending their rejection letters, the least they could do was buy him a burger.

A year later, *Cutting Edge* printed five of K'lyn's poems and Rob's story and sent them each two contributors' copies. Harry's lyrics came back with a polite rejection letter.

Truth or Fiction

ER WORDS CAME TRUE. AT first, Ruth thought it was coincidence. She wrote a story about an unexpected inheritance. A week later her uncle died, leaving her a thousand dollars in his will. Her character had won the money in a lottery, but wasn't death a lottery, equally fickle?

Ruth created a teenager, Ann, who wore too much eyeliner, dyed her hair blood-red, and collapsed on her seventeenth birthday from an overdose of Ecstasy on Electric Avenue in downtown Calgary. The next day, *The Herald* splashed pictures of Anne-Marie, her jagged red hair shocking against white bandages, being wheeled away from a nightclub. The headline read: Drugs Bring Down the Birthday Girl.

It was a close call. Anne-Marie survived, but Ruth was shaken. No more drugs, she told herself. No more death. Write happiness.

A week later, as she did on the first Sunday of every month, Ruth wrote a mystery for a women's magazine. It helped pay the bills. This time she wove a light plot revolving around a christening and a family secret. Birth equals happiness. Then she went to a christening for her cousin's infant son.

Over slices of cake with soft blue frosting, Ruth's second cousin and his wife erupted into a shouting match over the wife's infertility.

"If you hadn't had those two abortions in your twenties, we'd be pregnant."

"It's because you're shooting blanks. I never had this problem before."

She switched to the quirky, a waif named Toni who worked in a bookstore and wrote poetry. Ruth envied Toni's nose ring, clunky intellectual glasses, and bravado. She wanted to remake herself as Rue with a diamond stud, red hair, and boxy combat pants. But every winter she caught nasty colds, three weeks of inflamed sinuses and tissues heaping the garbage pail colds. Her hair dyed a muddy brown, never the Hawaiian sunset or burnt sienna the box promised. Combat pants made her feel fat. Toni faded into a wisp, blew away.

She started a postcard story about an older woman, a cheating boyfriend, settled on hair as a revenge motif, had Debbie (a 1980s name) stop by Tom's place with a bottle of Chivas Regal and a six-pack. When Tom passed out, Debbie took out some shears, snipped off his dirty-blond ponytail, collected a trophy. At a girls' night, Debbie pulled out the hair, laminated in a square of plastic, and drunkenly giggled, "That's not the only thing that was three inches."

Two days later, a local woman did a Lorena Bobbitt on her cheating boyfriend. His penis was three inches.

There was nothing Ruth could write about. She sat in her room, staring at her computer screen. Every word came laden with pain.

She went to a reading to see how other writers moved beyond this impasse. In a claustrophobic bar with black walls, she listened to fables about gangs of headhunters, about vampires in the flesh-pits of Bangkok, about haunted houses absorbing lonely seniors. A few smudged columns of type in any newspaper would reveal atrocities as unreal, love stories as strange, dreams as unlikely. Fact and fantasy blended together, a potent brew of "this is" followed by a "what if" chaser. She had dreamed it; therefore, it would come to pass.

She walked up to the stage, her hennaed hair gleaming, and took the microphone from the vampire writer, a faded woman whose hands were laden with clunky silver rings.

"Her words came true," Rue read. "The world swirls in possibilities that form as we articulate them. Writers legislate the universe. Words kill." She'd envisioned applause, but there was silence.

Rue whispered to the vampire woman, "Keep dreaming. The demon lover will appear. But then he will rip out your heart. Consider the consequences."

On her way home, she bought a pair of combat pants. No diamond stud. Variations are always possible.

The Heart Is a Red Apple

WHILE WAITING FOR HIM TO arrive, I eavesdrop on a conversation at the next table.

A thin girl in black, with cropped platinum hair and a diamond nose stud, complains to her green-eyed friend. "So I called my mom and told her. She was like, 'Do you want me to come up and beat him up? Because I will.' I said no. Then she asked if she should call me back, so I don't have a huge phone bill. And I said, 'I won't be here when it arrives.'"

"I can't believe you caught him," says the other woman. Multiple braids the colour of dried blood snake down her back.

"What I can't stand is the emails. He just left them there for me to see. He didn't even care that much. The whole thing seems so unreal to me, somehow. What was I thinking? Why did I let him treat me like that?"

The girls get up to leave just as he is coming in. He checks them out as they walk by, that not-too-subtle flicker of the eyes. The girls swivel past him, hipbones aggressively jutting from their low-cut jeans, bright orange thongs on display. I notice these things: the way the teenage cashier at the grocery store brightens in his presence; the way a server lingers, chatting, after he has paid the bill. I say nothing, but I do notice.

He puts his latte between us and says, "Tell me a story." Our daily ritual. I woo him with words. Wondering how I will hold him when that waif could not hold her lover, I weave a story of a bridge, of the links that bind separate sides into one.

The wooden bridge was once lined with railway trestles, a transportation link between north and south banks, ferrying lumber, coal, and food supplies. The iron rails were ripped up years ago, replaced with wooden boards. The bridge joins the two sides of the town, like the aorta of the heart, pumping life across the dark river.

On a windy spring day of freezing rain, two women walk the treacherous sidewalks. Rowan's hair swirls in long red tendrils around her aquamarine eyes. Her long cloak is the pale green of new grass. Men cross the street to avoid her shadow.

Dinar has platinum hair, cropped close as a boy's, and silver hoops chaining her ears. Above a black sweater and jeans, her face is pinched and white.

"My life is bleeding away," Dinar gasps. Under the skin of her wrist, a pulse jumps.

"Let him go, love," Rowan replies. "In his eyes, there is cruelty, in the thin line of his mouth. I have seen it."

"Can you tell the heart which path it should choose?"

"Come, it's cold. We must get home."

By evening the rain turns to sleet. The wind lashes the frozen branches of the trees in a frenzy. Dinar leans against the walls of their tower, staring out into the whirlwind.

"I see him in the glass," she cries, "embedded in my eyes. When I look out, he reflects back. He smiles and his fangs flash yellow light."

"Sleep. In the morning, you will feel better."

But in the morning, Dinar lies drained, her skin whiter than porcelain. "I dreamed of him. His voice dripped knives. He is in my veins and I cannot heal."

Rowan goes into the kitchen and finds a sharp paring knife. Wrapping herself in her cloak, her bright hair muffled by a scarf, she walks out into the storm.

When she knocks at his apartment, he is alone. He comes to the door, wearing jeans but no shirt. Plunging the knife into his chest, she parts lines of flesh and bone, cuts out his heart, takes it in her hand, a red apple.

Peering out into the storm, he asks, "Is anyone there?" Not noticing the drops of blood staining the threshold. Not noticing the empty space within his chest. He goes back inside, closing the door behind him.

Rowan walks home, blood from the dripping heart marking her trail. In the apartment, Dinar lies in bed, her chest barely rising and falling with each shallow breath.

"I have brought you his heart. Eat it and be well."

Dinar sits up. Clutching the heart in her white hand, so that red drops ooze between her fingers, she marvels, "It is so small."

"He didn't even notice it was gone."

"It is so cold."

"No colder than his eyes."

"It smells of rust and decay." She pushes back the sheet and stands up. "We will throw it in the river. His heart is worthless."

The wind blows from the south, smelling of warm earth and grass. Water flows down the sides of buildings in rivulets, the walls wavering and twisting in the pale light.

"Look," Rowan says. "There are green spears of daffodils in that sheltered corner."

The wooden bridge spans the river. Crossing to the centre, they throw the heart over the railing. Two women walk home hand in hand, the spring wind warm upon their faces.

"Is that a threat?" he asks. "Are you telling me what will happen if I stop showing up for coffee every day, if I stop listening to your stories?"

"A warning," I say. "My lover's eyes are sharp, and her knives are sharper. The heart is a valuable gift. One day I may ask her for yours."

He does not believe me. Men seldom do when you speak the truth. That is why I tell them stories.

Zoonis County

AROUND THE PERIMETER OF THE back yard, the maples droop. Dangling her legs over the edge of the peeling deck, Sara feels the uncut grass prickle against her shins. Voices float over her head. Evening mist. The taste of watermelon, slippery pits in her mouth mixed with rum. The heat pressing her down. A damp heat, so unlike dry prairie summers, sitting around the firepit in the evening with her cousins under a midsummer sky.

They're sharing first-time stories: first kiss, first time you had sex, first time you caught your parents having sex. Kelly, who is in her forties, talks about finding condoms in her son's dresser drawer.

She's been thinking about this story for twelve years. That summer she was seventeen, the year before university, the last year her cousins lived in Edmonton.

∽∽∽

On Saturday night after a shift at the bookstore, Sara rode her bike across the High Level Bridge to Zoonis County, a tiny decaying bungalow with concrete steps listing to one side. In the living room, a black-and-red-checked sleeping bag covered the futon, and posters of The Who and Deep Purple were thumbtacked to the walls. Messages in black marker were scrawled above the phone.

Sara sat down on the floor next to Jesse, wavy brown hair to his shoulders and bright blue eyes. He smiled lazily at her and passed the joint.

"Have you read *The Tibetan Book of the Dead?*" he asked. "The Tibetans believe that the soul doesn't leave the body for four days. So a guru stays with the body, prays over it, helps the soul leave." His voice was husky, confiding, so quiet that she had to lean in to hear him. Every word a secret. "The soul has to leave through the forehead. Like a camera shutter opening and closing."

Sara wanted to say something clever, but as so often with Jesse she just felt young and stupid. She couldn't tell him about what she was reading at school, *Animal Farm* and *Macbeth*. When he talked about Jackson Pollock and Henry Moore, she had to wait until she could go home and look up the names in an encyclopedia. So she just smiled and listened.

Jesse was six years older than her. He'd finished two years at the Ontario College of Art before dropping out and backpacking around southeast Asia: Thailand, Cambodia, Malaysia, Indonesia. A framed batik image of an Indonesian shadow puppet hung in his room in the basement: a crimson figure, hands held up in blessing, fingers touching thumbs.

At a midnight showing of *The Rocky Horror Picture Show*, Jesse started the crowd doing the time warp in line. They jumped to the left. They danced down 109th street into the Garneau Theatre. Inside, they'd thrown toast at the screen, held newspapers over their head when it rained, shouted "Boring" at the professor, screamed approval for the Rockys in gold lamé underwear and Magentas in busty black corsets in the costume show.

Jesse, Andrew, and Lynn had made the trip out west two years earlier in a rusty Dodge van and Jesse's '71 emerald Camaro. Jesse and Andrew worked in construction, along with Pete, Lynn's boyfriend. Lynn worked in a daycare. They'd come to Edmonton from Toronto in the boom years. The boom was over, but they were still here.

Time jerked forward in flipped records, beer bottles raised and lowered. The joint passed around the circle. No one talked except Pete, who was ranting about philosophy.

Sara looked over at Lynn, passed out on the floor. Lynn had low blood pressure and would frequently collapse during parties after her third or fourth beer. The first time it happened, Sara panicked, not sure if she should call an ambulance. But everyone else ignored Lynn, and Pete simply shifted her body so her head was resting on a cushion. Pete was a large man with a full brown beard. His voice grew louder and louder the more he drank, unlike Andrew who succumbed to silence, so that Pete would end the evening lecturing while Andrew slumped against the wall and Jesse smiled ironically, saying nothing.

Around midnight, she would leave, riding her ten-speed bike back over the bridge to her parents' house, the summer sky indigo, the moon a bright circle.

She always wondered what happened after she left. Did Pete carry Lynn to their bedroom? Did Andrew slump farther and farther over, a broken puppet, his strings cut? And Jesse. What did he do as the evening ticked down into the morning hours? Sometimes, when she left, other people would still be there, Lynn's friends from work, women with Farrah Fawcett wings,

women with bright red lipstick and thick streaks of blush on
their cheekbones, women who laughed too much and touched
Jesse too often, a confiding hand on his arm. Older women who
knew what they wanted.

At a party at Zoonis County to celebrate Solstice, the sun
high in the sky at eight, Sara walked into a room full of men
she didn't know, large men with Tom Selleck mustaches and
bushy dark beards.

Puff, a friend of Pete's, caught her eye. "So serious," he said.
"You're always so serious. Smile."

She slipped back to the kitchen, where Jesse was standing by
the fridge talking to one of Lynn's friends, Tracey, a tall woman
wearing a low-cut red shirt and acid-washed jeans. While
talking, she repetitively pulled her loose long hair back into a
ponytail, a move that pushed up her large breasts, shook the
blonde strands out in a crinkly mane, and then pulled her hair
back again, lifting the mane off the back of her neck.

"I'm so fucking tired. The brats kept us running today. I'd
just like to lay down for an hour's nap," she complained.

Sara caught the mistake and looked at Jesse to see if he'd
give her that sideways smile, that look he'd flash her when Pete
quoted Kierkegaard for the twentieth time in an argument. But
he was smiling at Tracey, an intense beam of concentration.

Sara leaned against the corner cupboard and drank her beer.
Beads of water dripped down the neck of the bottle, dampening
the label. She started peeling it back from a corner.

She had half the label peeled off, the smooth brown glass
of the bottle exposed, when Tracey looked over and smirked,
"If you can peel a label without ripping it, you're still a virgin."

Sara stopped peeling. She wanted to rip the label, but that felt stupid. Her face flushed.

"Hey, can you get me another beer if you're done?" Jesse winked at her.

Sara handed him a beer and went outside, sitting down next to Lynn, whose arms glowed taffy-brown against her white lacy top, a splash of turquoise blue in the hollow of her throat. She finished her beer, leaving the label untouched. Uncut twitch grass brushed against her legs. Lynn lit mosquito coils and the smoke rose straight up in the still air.

At two in the morning, someone suggested skinny-dipping in the fountain at the Legislature Grounds. Suddenly they were all moving, jumping out of the unpainted wooden chairs, dashing in a mad mob, flinging off shirts and shorts as they ran. Legs and bums shockingly white in the dusk, breasts and penises flopping, inhibitions shed, energy shimmering over their skin. Water on a hot night, that shock of cold against bare skin. Tracey screamed for attention as she raced away with the other streakers, her pendulous breasts exposed.

Sara wanted to join them, but the thought of being naked terrified her. She was frozen in her chair, watching everyone race out the back gate.

After they'd left, she sat alone for several minutes before going inside to the overly bright white kitchen. She ran icy water over her wrists, trying to clear the fuzziness in her head. No point in staying. Walking down the hall to get her purse, she opened Lynn's bedroom door, caught a glimpse of Jesse and Lynn entangled on the bed. The straps of Lynn's lacy top pushed down to her waist. The skin of her breast white against Jesse's tanned hands.

Sara backed out fast.

Another summer day of monotony at the bookstore punctuated by people treating her like an idiot. A girl had come in, thick black glasses, asymmetrical dyed black hair, very '80s New Wave.

"Do you have *The Fountainhead?*"

"By Ayn Rand?" Sara pronounced it Ann, never having heard the name spoken aloud.

"That's Aye-nn Rand," the woman drawled.

Yes, you fucking bitch, Sara thought, *and can you spell? Bookstores are arranged alphabetically. Rand would be under R.* She didn't say this. She wanted to keep her part-time $4.50 an hour job, especially since the manager would give her weekend hours once university started. So she smiled and led the pretentious bitch to the appropriate section.

At Zoonis County, her cousins lounged in a half-circle of lawn chairs in the back yard, a fenced area of knee-high grass and bright yellow dandelions, with a firepit in the centre. Slotting her Coke into a cooler full of ice, she sat down in a lawn chair with fraying green and white strips.

Lynn waved from across the circle. She was next to Pete, who was wearing his usual uniform of cargo shorts, with an Oilers cap hiding his receding hairline. Jesse and Andrew slouched in their chairs, in faded cutoffs and ripped T-shirts, beer bottles dangling from relaxed fingers.

By nine, the light had faded into a bloody sunset, red and orange streaks. Marianne Faithful growled about infidelity.

Pete came out of the back door. "We're out of beer," he said. No one responded.

"Did you hear me? We're out of beer," he said belligerently. "Which of you freeloaders drank my Coors?"

Everyone sprawled, silent.

"Fine, I'll get more myself." Pete headed to the back gate, slammed it shut.

"He's too drunk to drive." Lynn followed him. At the gate, she turned back. "Jesse, help me." Her shoulders and back glowed, bright red above her yellow tank-top. Jesse shrugged and pulled himself out of his chair. Sara hovered for a moment and then followed.

The van was parked in the back driveway, an unpaved area thick with dandelions. Pete was in the driver's seat, Jesse leaning over the open door, saying, "Listen to me. You're too drunk to drive."

"Give me my fucking keys."

"You're too drunk to drive."

"Fuck off."

"Get out of the damned van." Jesse grabbed Pete's shirt, pulled him out.

Pete fell awkwardly, jumped up, smashed Jesse against the door of the van, and punched him in the stomach, once, twice, and then swung at his head, missing as Jesse ducked. Sara watched from the gate, unable to move. Jesse splayed against the van, his arms held up protecting his head. Lynn screaming. "Pete, stop, Pete, stop."

Jesse, Lynn and Andrew were driving back east. Their construction jobs had ended, and the boom wasn't coming back.

"Might as well go back to school," Jesse told Sara. They were in his favourite coffee shop, Café la Guerre, sunk into one of the sagging brown sofas, drinking lattes from enormous blue mugs and sharing a piece of carrot cake with thick cream cheese frosting. Sara licked frosting off her fork, the sweetness aching in her teeth.

"I'll finish my degree. See if I can get some work doing illustrations. Publishing maybe. I want to do something creative."

Sara didn't know what she wanted to do with her life. University started in a week.

"Do you think you'll be out west next summer?" she asked.

"Doubt it." He smiled. "You'll have to come visit me. I'll show you some places."

"That would be awesome." But she knew it wouldn't happen.

Jesse died two months later. He rolled his Camaro on a gravel road near Peterborough. The car was totalled, but Jesse walked away unscathed. The next day he shot himself with his father's hunting rifle. The story was that he was sent home from the hospital with an untreated concussion.

The funeral was in Ontario. Sara and her mother flew east. A closed casket.

Lynn had hysterics just before the service started. She began hyperventilating, a wheezy breathing that sounded like a broken accordion, air forced through a bellows. Then she laughed, a shocking bark of sound.

Her friends led her to the back of the church, down a set of stairs to a wood-panelled room lined with black and chrome stacks of chairs. They hovered over her, patting her back, soothing her like a skittish horse. "It's okay, it was an accident."

For a few minutes, Sara watched Lynn's claim for attention, her desire to always be at the centre of events. Then she left. She couldn't go back into the funeral parlour. Climbing back out of that hot dark basement, she emerged into afternoon light, the grass glowing, brilliant green, even though it was November. She wandered under the dark shade of elms, their branches meeting in arches above her head.

∾∾∾

She tries to tell the story, but the fragments won't come together. Maybe if Jesse hadn't died young, he wouldn't be caught in a haze of summer light.

Some stories keep repeating. Two days ago, in a coffee shop, Sara saw a girl in bell-bottom jeans, a gossamer red top with butterfly sleeves, a gold chain. The past is haunting her, wearing her clothes. Does that girl sit in living rooms in decaying post-war houses, drink beer, long for someone unattainable?

Variations on a Theme

Beginnings

Sara has an eight-month teaching contract. She hadn't imagined that six years later she'd still be working on her dissertation, taking temporary contracts, moving every year to another town with the same vicious circles of intrigue and gossip. She'd had other plans, but now the patina of partial success clung to her, the faintest stale whiff, like cheap cologne.

David has black hair with a blue sheen, his eyes a dark glaze in a tanned face. When he smiles at Sara, her head is woozy from two quick glasses of cheap wine. They spin banter out of nothing. He goes outside to smoke a cigarette. When he comes back, he is stopped by a woman, small, bone-thin like a famine victim. She looks as if she would break in two if touched.

What Others See

"So what do you think of the new sessionals?"

"The usual. The disenchanted, the perpetually procrastinating, the failed writers. I was talking with Sara; she seems pleasant. She also seems very taken with David. I wonder if someone should warn her."

"It's like Frank and me. The first time we met, I knew what he was like. It doesn't matter what you know, you still do the same thing."

She tilts her head to one side, half-listening to familiar phrases. His relationship had ended four years ago but he is still rehashing the mistakes. Their conversation lulls into a familiar theme with variations, the andante section of a concerto, slow, measured, the same words falling over and over in slightly different patterns, building to the same crescendo.

"So I knew he was possessive, I mean for Christ's sake he told me to stop seeing my friends, an innocent hug in a restaurant and it was silence and cold shoulders for two, three days, but I kept thinking that I needed to be patient, to compromise for him. But you can't compromise yourself."

She's heard the phrase before. But smiles, nods. "No, you can't." Although isn't she doing just that, smiling and agreeing, when she should say, *It's been four years, move on, get over it.* But then who would listen to her complaints, ask for her tidbits of gossip, laugh at the bitter futility of the same dramas enacted over and over and over?

Constant Motion

At the end of a frustrating day of silent students, two endless meetings, and four hours of marking, Sara droops over her desk. Winter is approaching, another winter of closed doors and snowdrifts five feet high. Where will she be next year?

David stops by the door and asks, "What about a drink?"

Stephen Fearing's *The Assassin's Apprentice* plays over the hum of conversation in the bar. When the tiny fluttery server finally comes to rest beside them, he orders a beer and she asks for white wine, even though she wants vodka. She catches phrases seeping through the loudspeakers in Fearing's light tenor. David chain-smokes and tells her about his nearly finished novel.

"It's really a novel of ideas. Not like most of the work coming out in this country, banal little lives in mind-numbing detail. More like Don DeLillo. Have you read *White Noise?* Modern angst. Postmodern dislocations. I'm not into thumbnail realism. I want something bigger."

Are people still "into" things, she wonders, noticing her attempted distance, the implied criticism. She doesn't say this. Instead she smiles, nods, admires the way his turquoise shirt brings out a warm sheen in his soft brown skin, the way he pauses and looks off into the distance, thoughtfully, as he drags on his cigarette. A certain lack of self-awareness or a pose so practised it looks instinctive.

"But do things ever really end?" she asks, after he uses the phrase "postmodern lack of closure" for the third time.

"No, exactly. That's what I'm saying. Nothing ever really ends; it's all endless repetitions, the same stories over and over. A feed-back loop."

"Like at the end of the movie *Speed*," she blurts out, regretting instantly as the words slip away. Why that movie, that reference? Inarticulate Keanu Reeves and the mass market appeal of a continuously moving bus. Constant motion, the postmodern metaphor. She files the thought away for a possible paper topic.

"I don't see the connection." He stares over her shoulder, his eyes unfocused, and now she feels a brief spurt of anger for his dismissal. No doubt he only watches grainy foreign films, with subtitles.

"It's not important." An uncomfortable pause and she starts talking department gossip.

They leave the golden dim of the bar. A light snow is falling, gentle flakes drifting down, illuminated by the old-fashioned street lights enclosing the public square. A night for lovers. She reaches for his left hand. It is icy cold. "Cold hands, warm heart," she jokes. His hand hangs, boneless, inert within her grasp, but she cannot let go now.

Friday night sex in his office, the hard edges of the desk against her thighs, their clothing abandoned at their feet. The door left partially ajar.

What People Talk About

"Why does she put up with him?"

"I don't know. Maybe she has low self-esteem. She doesn't believe she deserves to be treated with respect."

"So what's the latest gossip?" He scoops up the foam on the side of the cup with a plastic spoon and licks the cinnamon-flecked white cloud, a pink flick of tongue. Vaguely obscene.

She looks down, grimaces. "Oh, I don't like to say."

"Come on, tell. You can't just start something and leave it hanging."

"Well, they're still together. I think. But last week I saw him after work, at Play It Again, having a beer. With that woman from his department. You know, the one who is so thin she looks anorexic."

"Does Sara know?" he asks, avidly curious for the latest development in this soap opera.

"I don't know. Maybe not. David has always been like that."

"Are you going to tell her?"

"Do you think I should?"

What We Leave Behind

Folding clothes, Sara finds one of his shirts and wishes she'd found it before the smoky burn of tobacco washed from the weave, before his smell was obliterated by the cool perfume of laundry detergent. She rubs the black cotton against her face, imagining his cheek, rough with unshaven stubble, his hands cold against her neck.

His hands were always cold. She'd bought him gloves at Christmas, thinking of Tristan and Iseult. The king's words to Iseult — *Your hands are cold, but I will warm them* — the glove placed on the breast of the sleeping Iseult. She couldn't share the reference, any mention of love forbidden. They lived within the tight lines of his comfort zone.

Wearing Masks

"So I was walking by Sara's office this afternoon and I could tell she'd been crying."

"What did you do?" he asks.

"I stopped in and asked if she was okay. She was embarrassed, but I wanted her to know she has a friend, someone she can confide in. But she said she was fine."

"I didn't think you were that close."

"Well, we're not really, but it helps to have someone to talk to."

"You just wanted the dirt."

He knows her too well. She smiles, acknowledging the hit. Around him, glimpses of her other self peer out, not just the carefully constructed persona: the confident professor, the aging woman. How soon until she metamorphoses into a wise, old crone?

"I do have some gossip," she confides. "A colleague told me David was seen leaving that woman's apartment on Monday morning. You know, the skinny one."

"What is he doing, notching his bedpost with every woman on campus? You'd think he'd have learned; you can't hide anything here. You found that out your first year."

"Yes. Just like I found out Frank was cheating on you, before you knew."

He flinches, and then gazes reproachfully at her, but she refuses to feel guilty. He alluded to her past, a taboo topic, those few weekends with David. His coldness. Her mask of indifference.

The Only Cure is Distance

The university offers another contract, but Sara refuses, accepts another job. The town is too small for two of them, only a few bars and one university, she can't escape, too many people know. There are too many opportunities to walk past his apartment, phone his number, casually introduce his name into conversation. It hurts too much. She has to leave.

Packing up her dishes, she remembers meals together. Feeding him ravioli with her fingers, the sauce smearing his mouth. When she straddled him on the chair, kissing him, her lips wide, tongue probing, he tasted of tomato and garlic, a warm oregano-scented flavour with a hint of iron and blood.

In bed the next morning, she kissed his stomach, down the thickening line of dark hair, his skin warm and sweaty, garlic and oregano and sex on the tongue.

No, not that memory. Replace it. The chocolate cake with rum icing she'd baked for his birthday, and he showed up two hours late, smelling of stale beer and cigarettes.

"Who were you with?"

"Just friends, okay. Just a few birthday drinks."

"I've been waiting." She hated the whine of fear and anger in her high-pitched voice.

"You said eight. It's not that late. Jesus, don't turn possessive on me."

Bloodshot eyes, five o'clock shadow. See the flaws, see the flaws, but she couldn't, the hooks too deep, and she softened, forgiving, just a few drinks with friends, what could that hurt, and no, he hadn't been with that woman again, he'd promised, she would ignore the rumours whispered into her ear by poisonous tongues.

The dish smashes on the cracked linoleum of the kitchen floor. She will wrench herself free, move again, leaving behind yet another shallow pool of acquaintances, another closed circle of intrigue and gossip. Another circle of pain.

Different Endings

"Do you ever wish for a different ending? You look back and all you remember are the things you've done that you're ashamed of." He holds up his cup helplessly.

She thinks of her actions. A few carefully planted words and David is alone again. Victory tastes of burnt ashes and stale cold coffee, but there is nothing else left.

Homesick

S HE COULD HAVE MET ANYONE: a Buddhist, a sculptor, a *yakuza*.

Only flashes of her first few days remain. Tired, awed, anxious, she'd floated through the drive from the airport. The overwhelming impression was grey, interspersed with flashes of green. *Wizard of Oz* green. Flat paddy fields swirled into spaghetti highway ramps and multi-storey apartment buildings rising higher and higher as they drove into the multiple layers of Tokyo.

In the reception area of the Shinjuku Hyatt Hotel, the English teachers milled around the grand piano, their luggage in untidy piles on the marble floor. Maya stared up at glittering glass chandeliers shaped like floating jellyfish. The lobby was open to the fourth floor and voices rose and fell in a whirlpool of sound. Solitary emissaries from the government, laden with enormous red ribbons as if they'd been awarded Best in Show, swam through the shoals, dropping questions like bait.

"*Nihon wa, doh desu ka?*" What do you think of Japan?

"*Kirei desu.*" It's beautiful.

She wakes to *shoji* screens rattling in their frames, china clattering on the shelves. The floor heaves, unstable as a fun house. Staggering across the room, Maya clutches the door frame.

The quake stops. Hands shaking, Maya picks up the phone, dials Kim's number.

"*Moshi, moshi.* Kim speaking."

"Kim, it's Maya. Did you feel that?"

"What, the earthquake? It was just a baby. Maybe a 4.5. We've had quakes like that in Vancouver. It won't even make the news. Don't worry — it's not the big one."

Kim gets her laughing about the twins, Jack and Bill (Kim calls them Jack and Jill), and how they drank too much at a party in a Tsuchiura restaurant and recited Monty Python skits for an hour. Maya can't believe she met Kim only two weeks ago.

Kim and Maya catch a ride to an English conference with one of the teachers from Kim's school. Hukaya-sensei is shy, thirty-four, unmarried. His English is good but formal, a bit stilted. Kim speaks Japanese. Maya watches the countryside go by: weathered wooden houses with gargoyles guarding the corners of the tiled roofs; pachinko parlours, their enormous neon signs blinking pink and orange above the glass-fronted entrances. The roads are narrow with deep ditches. In the fields, golden-brown sheaves of rice hang over triangular wooden frames to dry, like books propped open on their spines.

Maya hears English being spoken and for a moment it's a foreign language, low-pitched and liquid.

"We're being rude," Kim is saying. "Maya doesn't speak Japanese."

"No, I'm the typical Canadian *gai-jin*." Maya tries to make a joke of it. "I didn't even know how to pronounce *Hajimemashite* back in July when I arrived. My students corrected me."

"Oh really," he responds, the intonation exactly like that of her students, slightly disbelieving. As if he is too polite to contradict her.

The hotel is a modern, twelve-storey building, on the edge of the resort town. In their room, Elaine, an older woman, sprawls out on a futon, reading *Wild Swans*.

"Hi." She waves a hand. "Welcome to Hotel Mashiko. Such a lovely place. Futons laid out with a corner folded back just so."

As always, Maya notices how big Elaine is, how exuberant. How insignificant she makes her feel.

"I'm going to find the *onsen*." Kim pulls a lime-green *yukata* out of her knapsack. "This hotel is famous for its underground pool. One of the three best in Tochigi," she chirps, and Elaine and Maya laugh. It's a standard phrase in Japan guidebooks. One of the three best waterfalls in Hokkaido, one of the three best parks in Tokyo. Kim calls her apartment, next to a train station, one of the three noisiest apartments in Japan.

The bath is segregated, men and women. In the antechamber, a small room with shelves of pink baskets, they undress.

"I hope it's not crowded," Elaine says. "I get so tired of everyone staring at the big fat *gai-jin*. God, I need to lose some weight." She grabs a handful of the roll at her stomach.

The underground *onsen* circles a tiny island thick with ferns. Naked children splash at the edges of the grotto, watched over by mothers with their pubic hair modestly concealed by white washcloths. Elaine wades over to the far edge of the pool where they are partially shielded from the *obaasans*, the tiny grandmothers with grey hair and disapproving frowns. They sink down on the bench that rims the island, steaming water covering their shoulders.

"So how's Mick," Elaine asks Kim. Kim's boyfriend, Mick, is staying with Japanese friends in Tokyo, looking for a job. Her school board asked him to leave when they found out he was living in Kim's apartment.

"He hasn't found a job yet. And forget apartments in Tokyo. Ten thousand yen a month and you have to pay the key fee on top of that. It's so unfair," Kim says bitterly. "I can think of three guys who have their girlfriends openly living with them. Plus, one of the math teachers is married to a former student. Yeah, that's really appropriate."

Maya leans back against the island, its concrete edge rasping her shoulders. Her legs are turning the soft pink of cooked shrimp. She closes her eyes and imagines herself at the Banff Hot Springs, hearing the high-pitched giggles from children, smelling sulphur and chlorine. Her shoulders and neck relax, the heat massaging out tension. Then she opens her eyes, and the illusion vanishes in the dimness of the grotto filled with naked women.

The next morning, at a lecture on English games, Maya sits down beside a tall man with curly brown hair and horn-rimmed glasses. In his dark-blue suit, white shirt, and sober tie in swirls of navy and emerald green, he seems to be the only Western adult in the room. Most of the other men (half-hatched between college and career) wear casual cotton slacks and polo shirts or shorts and sweatshirts. She and Eric compare schools afterwards.

"My school is awful," he says. "They don't care because they don't have a chance in hell of getting into university. So they just piss around in class. A couple of weeks ago, these two Yankee boys, you know the ones with dyed orange hair, started fighting. And before Mr. Onuma, he's the Japanese teacher, could get to them, the bigger kid pushed the other out the window. From the second floor."

"Was the kid hurt?" Maya asks, shocked.

"No, just some bruises."

She can't reciprocate with her own horror stories. Her students are serious, hard-working, university bound. Another world.

They eat supper together in a large tatami room, up a step from the hallway littered with a tangle of abandoned sneakers and backless hotel slippers. Maya sits cross-legged on a cushion before a wooden tray, with Kim on one side and Eric on the other. Elderly women in dark kimonos dish up rice from steaming iron cauldrons. Geometric patterns form on the trays: deep blue bowls filled with pale thick *udon* noodles; twisted pieces of pink rubbery octopus; layers of fried vegetable tempura on an octagon-shaped plate with a side platter of soy.

"I wish they'd serve something edible," Elaine bitches, as she hands plate after plate across the table to Eric. "About the only thing I like is the rice."

"Look, custard with a surprise," Kim spoons out a piece of shrimp.

Eric asks, "So where are you from?"

"Calgary. I got my degree at the U of C," she says. "I wanted to go to Toronto or Montreal, but my parents said I should get my first degree at home. I don't know; it seems the Canadian way. Most people I talk to got their degree in their hometown."

"Not like the Americans," he agrees. "They get together and all they can talk about is which college is better-rated."

"Where did you go to school?" Maya asks. She focuses on Eric, on his eyes, a light brown with a yellow edge around the pupil; the way his nose crooks a bit to the left side; his voice, pitched low and soft so she has to lean in a little to hear him.

"UBC, of course. In psych. Perfect training for living in Japan."

They talk about watching the Canucks, spring skiing at Whistler, sushi in Vancouver restaurants, his summer job on a salmon boat, and all the time Maya hears her own longing for home twisting through his words like a silver ribbon.

After supper, they walk out into the dark streets of the resort town, a carefully preserved remnant of feudal Japan: cobblestone streets lined with closely set shops, a dark patina of age on their wooden exteriors; the crisp autumn air smelling of pine; stars shining overhead, a low yellow moon. When Kim and Elaine turn a corner, Eric pushes Maya up against a wooden wall and kisses her, his hands pulling hard on her hips. Splinters rasp through the rough weave of her sweater.

"Eric never shuts up, does he," Kim says later that night, sprawled out on one of the four futons covering the floor.

"I think he's just homesick." Maya opens the French doors and goes outside. The balcony looks over a narrow ravine and she can see the hotels lining the other side, square blocks of golden light marking the lines of windows. A creek murmurs far below.

"Look, Kim, you can see the stars." She hadn't seen them since she'd arrived in Japan.

Eric phones Tuesday night after the conference and they agree to meet for coffee in Mito. He drives up from Yaita, an hour's trip.

She can't decide what to wear. Jeans seem too informal, but her navy business suit is too structured. She tries on a short black skirt paired with lacy black T-shirt and outlines her mouth in red lipstick, Cover Girl's Perfect Passion. Staring into the mirror, she sees a pale child, white skin, dark hair, the lipstick a slash of colour. A wisp of fairy tale rhyme slips through her mind: skin as white as snow, lips as red as blood. Maya scrubs off the lipstick with a tissue, takes off her glasses and puts on blue mascara and her contact lens.

At the Mito clock, Maya sits down on a bench in front of a raised flower bed, the golden chrysanthemums looking bedraggled in the crisp chill of late fall. Around her, the crowds of salarymen in suits and schoolchildren in plaid uniforms surge in and out of the station's glass doors, across the wide pedestrian bridge, and down the stairs onto the main street of the city.

A neatly dressed woman stops in front of her.

"Excuse me, do you speak English?" she asks.

"Yes," says Maya. Another person wanting to practise English conversation with a foreigner. They always target her. She hopes Eric will arrive soon and rescue her. But rather than the usual questions about where she is from and what are her hobbies, the woman asks, "May I pray over you?"

"Umm." What kind of weird request is this? The actions of the sarin cult flash into Maya's mind. Had they prayed over people?

"Just for a moment," the woman insists. She looks respectable in her straight blue skirt and white blouse. In fact, she could be a clone of the two girls, also in white blouses and straight short skirts, calling out "*Dozo, dozo*" as they hand out packets of tissues with the name of an English conversation school on the plastic wrapping. Maya looks around. There are enough people passing by that she should be safe.

"Okay," she says, taking a tighter hold of her knapsack. "Only for a minute."

"Just a minute," the woman agrees. "Please to close your eyes."

Maya closes her eyes. She expects chanting, but there is silence. Then a tingling starts in her scalp, as if the woman is holding her hands just a few inches from Maya's hair. It feels like having her hair brushed by her mother when she was little. Maya feels the gentleness of her mother's hands as she slowly pulls the brush through the long black hair, carefully untangling the tats. The tingling passes down into her shoulders, relaxing tension in the muscles, the walls she has erected deep in her body. Then the hands lift and there is an empty space at the top of her head. Maya opens her eyes.

"*Domo arigato gozaimasu.*" The woman bows deeply, turns, and walks back towards the train station.

When Eric arrives, she takes him to her second-favourite coffee shop, rather than her "number one" place where the owner, a mid-thirties man with a penchant for printed polyester shirts, frequently gives her free coffee.

"*Irrashaimasu,*" call the men behind the counter as they walk in. A group of schoolgirls in the navy pleated skirts and jackets of Mito Nikko, her high school, look over and giggle, covering their mouths with their hands. Maya smiles and waves. She'll be pestered with questions about her boyfriend all next week.

Maya orders two *kohi kreamus.* "It's the closest thing you'll get to a latte outside of Tokyo," she tells him as they sit down at a table in the back corner of the shop.

"I've only been to the Mr. Donut here. The one on the other side of the street."

"Where they play American radio all day?"

"This is Casey Cassum, coming at you with another golden oldie." Eric sings Elvis's "Hound Dog" in a deep baritone. The students in the corner turn. Eric waves at them and they blush and look away.

She meets him the next night. They spend the weekend together at her apartment.

"I love your shoulders," she says, stroking her hands over the soft skin, the outlined muscles. They sit on cushions on her living room floor, CD cases scattered over the tatami, half-empty mugs of tea resting on pieces of newspaper so they won't leave rings on the floor.

"I love your hands," holding one of his big hands between hers, biting the fingers gently, running her tongue down the creases between the fingers. How can she explain the sudden pull that flares between them, rising out of nowhere, the *have to see him* urgency?

They drive to a party at Kim's house. Eric has drunk a couple of beers and she has to drive. Road signs flash by them, beautiful sharp lines of kanji looking like chicken wire, tangled and incomprehensible, as they follow winding narrow roads down the coast. At an intersection, Maya doesn't know whether to go left or right. White sedans flow steadily in both directions.

"I think it's a right here," Eric says, consulting the crudely drawn map. Maya swears. Right means a turn across traffic into the far lane.

"Pull out a little. You'll never get turned."

Maya ignores him.

"You should have gone." A brief gap appears, and then fills quickly.

She can feel his impatience and the frustration of the drivers behind her like a pile of wet cement in her chest. She switches the blinker to the left and pulls out too fast, with a squeal of tires, behind an ancient truck piled high with vegetables.

"You're going the wrong way."

"Just shut up and let me drive," Maya spits back, breathless with anger.

He shuts up. She turns off the main road at a pear orchard, the trees dark and bare behind their blue netting, takes the next right and finds a secondary road that looks familiar. After another twenty minutes of sulky silence, in which Eric refuses to give any directions at all, they arrive. He spends the evening flirting with two Japanese women in mini-skirts and thigh-high stockings.

They fight the same fights, when she is tired and hungry, less willing to be accommodating. Fights that they resolve with her hand on his arm, tentative, asking. His lips against hers, the scratchiness of five o'clock stubble rasping her skin, scrubbing away uncertainties.

She becomes hypersensitive about touch. Her students giggle when she demonstrates how to shake hands; a girl bursts into tears when Maya tries to make her shake hands with a boy. With adults, Maya bows quickly and waits to see if they bow back or want to shake hands. Yet there are hostess bars cluttering the blocks around the train station; salarymen on the train openly read pornographic comics about schoolgirls.

She breaks up with Eric by telephone. Broken up, broken apart. Those few weeks together fall like shattered glass on the tatami, lodge under her fingers like blisters.

"Did you see the problems?" she asks Kim. She wants Kim's answer to comfort her. Kim never liked Eric.

"Look, Maya, what does it matter?" Kim finally says. "Six months from now you'll be gone and you'll never have to see him again. It was just a fling, right?"

That thought haunts her even more.

Fractures

THEY FLEW TO TOKYO FROM Vancouver, but nothing was the same. "Last time, I flew business class on JAL," Maya told Brent. "We had free movies, free kiwi juice or champagne, California rolls for lunch, *udon* in clear broth, tuna sashimi."

This time her TV didn't work. She'd given Brent the window seat, but he fell asleep after the first meal and didn't wake until they landed in Narita. The airport was obscured by clouds.

When she was a child, her mother had told her stories about Urashima the Fisherman, trapped below the waves. When he returned home, one hundred years had passed, his family had died, and life was strange to him. She was returning to Japan ten years later, expecting everything to be the same.

They stayed in the Sakura hostel for two days and wandered around Ueno Park where the homeless camped out in blue tents. In the Kappa Bashi district, stores sold plastic models of sushi and *donburi* for restaurant displays. One display showed pieces of orange and purple plastic sushi arranged to mimic Munch's *The Scream*.

"This isn't the authentic Japan," she told Brent. "When we get out in the countryside, that's real."

"You sound like that woman we met at the JET reunion. Nadine. Raving on about how Kyushu was the only 'authentic' Japan, how she studied *zazen* with a Buddhist monk. What makes one experience more authentic than another?"

On the third day, they took the train north to Mito, where she had taught at a senior high school for two years. Walking out of the echoing cave of the train station, they crossed the overpass into downtown. In the first two blocks she counted off the landmarks: the coffee shop where she'd been greeted with cries of *urashai*; the flower shop with its bucket of vivid yellow roses and crimson zinnias; the French restaurant and her favourite bar; the zoom and bustle of main street, all unchanged. Turning north, they strolled through a downtown park lined with chestnut trees, thick green leaves dappled with late-summer sunshine, two older women exercising their Akitas in the wide-open grassy bowl.

After a left turn, they walked four blocks until they came to a high brick wall that stretched for half a block. The school. The iron gates stood open, leading into a circular drive in front of the three-storey school.

The courtyard was gone. In its place, at right angles to the old wooden school, stood an annex of steel and concrete.

"It's gone. They've cut down all the trees." Loss gripped her. The garden had sheltered the east side of the school. Up on the third floor, she felt like Rapunzel, locked in a tower. Maple trees and cedars, a patterned forest of red and emerald green, had shaded the winding paths. A secret garden with a brick wall, barely visible through the thick leaves. In October, the maple trees outside the window glowed, each leaf etched in crimson points of exquisite origami.

Stopping at Daie's grocery store on the way back, Maya bought a pre-packaged selection of sushi: barbequed eel, salmon draped in silvery pink strips over rice, *kappa maki*. She ate it on the street, scooping up pieces with her fingers, dipping the sushi in soy sauce, ignoring the frowns of disapproval from people walking by. She didn't live here now. She didn't have to follow their rules.

That night they went to a festival at the Kasama Shrine to honour the beginning of the Fall Grand Sumo Tournament. Maya had seen the shrine once before, during the October chrysanthemum festival, when the area glowed with yellow, purple, and white mums in pots and samurai figures sculpted in blossoms with flat papier-mâché faces. They walked past rows of fox statues carved from grey stone, their red cloth bibs a flash of colour, making them look like children's story animals about to sit down to a buffet.

Twisted rope, thick as a weight-lifter's arm, hung from one side of the entrance to the other. Lightning bolts of white paper zigzagged down the rope. Under the heavy curves of the roof, with corners cupped like hands held out for rain, the interior of the shrine loomed, an empty sacred presence. Before the shrine hung a large copper bell to summon the gods.

"Ring the bell and then clap your hands three times," Maya instructed Brent. "You can ask favour of the gods." She demonstrated, swinging the wooden post against the bell, clapping her hands, and then bowing her head in prayer. But she could think of nothing to ask.

Behind the shrine, hundreds of people jostled together, trying to get close to a wooden stage. It felt like a rock concert, the press of expectant bodies, the good-natured jostling, the reverential air.

The wrestlers paraded out, dressed in formal black kimono, and were blessed by the priests. And then the wrestlers bent down over sacks, like darkly clad Santa Clauses, and began hurling things at the crowd. Items flew through the air. Instant cameras. Ichiban packages. Green tea. Bags of fish-shaped crackers. Triangles of *onigiri*, wrapped in clear plastic.

She was hemmed in by bodies and it was raining Ichiban. Packages fell to either side of her, like unexploded bombs. People stretched their hands above her, like fans at a ball game waiting to catch the foul ball, the pop fly. The crowd pressed closer and closer to the stage. The hail of gifts spread in a net above her head.

An Ichiban package struck Maya's forehead above the left eye, just missing her glasses. Stars flashed. She put her hand up, too late to protect herself.

Brent grabbed her shoulder. "Maya! Are you okay?"

Maya took her hand away from her forehead. "I'm okay. It isn't cut." There was only a slight pulsing ache above her eye.

"Let's get out of here. These crowds are insane."

On the trip back to Mito in the brightly lit commuter train, she swayed back and forth, surrounded by salarymen red-faced with sake. She was woozy, as if she were seeing the landscape through only one eye, in two dimensions. A flat stage. Disconnected. Raising a hand to her forehead, she touched the small hard bump on the left side above her eye, still red and sore. In the novel *The Makioka Sisters*, the second sister, Yukiko, develops a brown patch above one eye, a sign of spinsterhood. Would the bump leave a scar? Had Japan reached out and tattooed her forehead?

The next day, they travelled south. She was most comfortable in transit, on buses, planes, trains, shuttling between points. In constant motion, she didn't have to solidify into one person. Looking out the train windows, she saw bright-green rice fields. The flat mirror of the window reflected her back. No sign of the fractures within. Past. Present. Her old self from ten years earlier, all those lost dreams.

They stopped at Himeji Castle, *Haruko-jo*, the White Egret, built in 1580 by Toyotomi Hideyoshi. Crossing the moat into the castle, they followed one-way arrows through twisting stone mazes of defence. Inside, the maze became horizontal, stairs morphing into wooden ladders, higher and higher through the six levels, until they ascended through trap doors. Rooms shrank, the ceiling fell. Maya watched Brent's muscular legs as she held onto the rope on either side of the wooden stairs.

Climbing back down, Maya froze.

"Maya? What's the matter?"

The rope bit into her palms. She couldn't let go. A wave of dizziness spilled over her as the room spun in circles.

"Nothing. Just stopped to catch my breath." She closed her eyes. Her left foot hung in the air, suspended over nothingness. She breathed deeply and reached down. Her foot jarred against the rung, anchoring her in space.

In the garden outside, she slumped on a stone bench, winded. Her head was still spinning. Brent smoked a cigarette and then flicked the stub into the water. Behind a veil of green willow branches, the moat gleamed red with fire as the sun set.

The hill back to the train station was lined with restaurants and shops. They walked past open doors, each with the owner standing in the opening, calling *Irrashai!* Welcome.

At a souvenir booth, she bought a gift. Inside a decorative box patterned with flying cranes was a mirror the size of her palm. On its back, painted on delicate cream paper, a plum tree with white blossoms. Like the decorated *omiyage* sweets, too beautifully wrapped to eat, her emotions were wrapped in paper, stored away like a kimono for the proper season. Was she feeling nostalgia or dread? She didn't know.

On the hill behind her, *Himeji-jo* was lit with white light, a white heron unfolding multiple wings in flight.

At a love hotel, a façade of turrets and battlements, they chose a space age room with silver walls, silver shag carpet, a blue bedspread sprinkled with stars. They paid for the room through a vending machine in the tiny impersonal lobby: 4000 yen for three hours, 6,500 for the night.

"God, I'm beat." Brent threw himself down on the bedspread, his runners still on.

"You should take off your shoes."

"Maya, do you know how many stains are on this bedspread? My shoes aren't going to hurt it."

"Take off your damned shoes. It's disrespectful."

Sighing heavily, Brent sat up, unlaced his runners, and then tossed them into a corner of the room. "Happy now?"

She lay back against the bedspread. Glow-in-the-dark stars patterned the ceiling. The Big Dipper. Cassiopeia's Chair. When she closed her eyes, she saw luminescent stars.

"I don't know what's going on," she said. "I thought it would be the same as before. I feel like a stranger."

Brent said nothing.

"I'm sorry about the shoes," Maya said. "That was stupid. I just keep remembering all the rules. *Don't hold hands in public. Don't pour your own drink. Don't wear your shoes indoors. Don't eat while walking.* The rules shouldn't apply to me now. I don't live here. But they're in my head." She reached over and touched his hand in apology. She wanted to share her experience of Japan with him. But nothing was as she'd planned.

"That's okay. We climbed a lot of stairs today. You're tired."

"Maybe." She couldn't tell him how she really felt. It was as if she wasn't really there. As if everything was happening to someone else.

"Hiroshima tomorrow. We should get some sleep." Brent took off his T-shirt and shorts, dumping them by the sneakers. He crawled back into bed and stretched his arm behind her head. After a few moments, he was asleep.

Maya lay still, listening to his deep breathing.

She hadn't travelled further than Himeji Castle the first time. Too expensive. Now with the JAL passes available only to foreigners, they boarded the *shinkansen* to Hiroshima. Insulated from the world outside, they arrived in less than three hours.

Storing their knapsacks at the train station, they explored the gardens of the Hiroshima Peace Memorial Park, snapping pictures of statues draped with rows of multi-coloured origami cranes. In her junior-high English class, Maya had taught the story of Sadako Sasaki, the girl of a thousand cranes. According to a Japanese legend, anyone who folded a thousand origami cranes would be granted a wish. Diagnosed with leukemia in 1954, nine years after the atomic bomb was dropped on her home, Sadako folded over a thousand cranes, some from medicine wrappers and gift paper. She died at the age of twelve.

Tourists were everywhere, in pairs, in families, and in groups led by Japanese women in suits, carrying umbrellas. The buzz of many languages filled the air.

Maya and Brent flowed with the crowds into the museum. In the main hall, a giant black sphere hung above a topographical map of Hiroshima. The time the bomb was dropped — 8:15 — flashed in red letters on the sphere.

Upstairs, a claustrophobic brick hallway led into a room of glass cases filled with artifacts. Watches stopped at exactly 8:15. A finger joint. A mannequin dressed in the recovered school uniforms of three teenagers.

In the corner of the room were the pink and grey stones of a wall and steps from a bank. She saw the shadows of the dead imprinted on the wall. Ghosts attached to time by the thinnest of threads.

Vertigo spun her around. The room blurred. Maya grabbed Brent's hand. "I have to go back outside."

In the sunlight of the Peace Garden, her dizziness passed. Maya sat down on a bench in front of a bed of orange and yellow chrysanthemums. "That black sphere looked like the Death Star," she said, trying to grab control of her emotions. The wrong thing to say. Fortunately, only Brent was near her.

On the way back to the train station, they stopped at a Starbucks for iced coffee. Sitting at a table, Maya looked out the glass windows at a modern city: hotels, apartment buildings, 7-11s, shops, divided main streets, all untouched. The fragments didn't fit together. She was left with bits of memory. A few moments defined a life. A piece of clothing. A stopped watch.

The Eater of Dreams

1. *Gai-jin* Ghost

It was O-Bon, the three days in mid-August when the dead return, when I noticed the draft.

I was lying on my futon, wearing nothing but a tank top and underwear, feeling the steamy sauna heat stick to my skin. I couldn't tell where the cold draft on my neck came from: the window was closed, and the air blowing from the fan was as hot and humid as the air in the rest of the room.

Woke up at three in the morning and saw a grey shape in the corner of the bedroom. Grey mist. Drifted back to sleep, convinced I'm dreaming.

Noise outside my window wakes me again. Opening the faded blue curtains, I see lines of telephone wires criss-crossing a hazy sky. Loudspeakers hang from a pole right outside the window — that's where the music is coming from, if you can call it music. I'd call it other things: a cat being tortured, a record played at 78 rpm, the Chipmunks on a kazoo. Two stories down an elderly man on a bicycle careens down the claustrophobic street lined with grey concrete apartment blocks. Where are the shrines and temples, where are the cherry trees with their transient beauty, where are the geishas in brightly embroidered kimono, where are the shining neon signs of Ginza, where are the green rice fields and misty hills? Where is the Japan the writers promised me?

The bedroom encloses me, a hot humid box. Tatami mats, yellow squares lined with leaf-green borders, smelling of stale straw and dust, cover the floor. In the corner is a tiny wooden table, only two feet off the ground, with two cushions piled under it. Sliding *shoji* screens, wooden frames with paper squares, separate the rooms: one white square has a jagged hole in it, the size of a fist. My first day here, I bashed my head on the screen's frame, which is only five feet high. I feel like Gulliver in the land of the Lilliputians. Like Alice in Wonderland. Oversized and monstrous. Jefferson Airplane runs through my mind. I've gone down the rabbit's hole, a nine-thousand-mile free fall to the other side of the world.

Beside the futon is a pile of information books: language primers, *The Lonely Planet Guide to Japan*, the JET orientation book. I open one at random. *Amaterasu O Mikami, the divine mythical ancestor of the Japanese imperial family, was the daughter of the creator gods, Izanagi and Izanami. Angered by her brother's behaviour, she hid in a cave, plunging the earth into darkness. The Japanese people believe she came out of the cave when she saw her reflection in a mirror.* What will I see?

I peel myself off the sweaty futon, my back stiff and sore, and wander into the empty kitchen. Sean, the teacher before me, stole the dishes, pots, sheets, towels, furniture. I'm surprised he left the lightbulbs. He got a job at an English school in Tokyo after a year here. The school board is supposed to kick in ten thousand yen for supplies, but it will be a cold day in Ibaraki before I see that money.

I pour myself some orange juice and sit down on my one remaining chair. At least I'm off the floor. My third morning here I woke up, bleary-eyed, pissed off at the Edelweiss song on the loudspeaker, stumbled into the kitchen barefoot and saw it. A cockroach. I grabbed a paper and started flailing madly away. Swat, swat, swat, the cockroach scurrying frantically for the edge of the room, swat, swat, I got it, but then the damned thing wouldn't die. It kept crawling and I'm whacking away at it, *whack, whack,* yelling "Die, you sucker, die." Finally, it was lying on the tatami, this shiny black blob, waving its legs because it still wasn't dead, so I got my runner and hit it a few more times. I've found some cockroach killers in the cupboard, small cardboard boxes with a picture of a happy cockroach (probably drunk on sake) crawling in, then getting stuck in the sticky paper. Like me. I was drawn in by the sweet smell of yen. Now I'm stuck, waving my legs in the air.

My supervisor picks me up at eight. She's been driving me to school each day, until they can replace the bicycle that Sean stole. Kawabata-sensei reminds me of a prison warden with her stiff black suits and stiffer smile. I climb into the white Toyota, wondering what the hell we'll talk about today. She has a topic already chosen.

"In Japan," she says, "we eat rice rather than potatoes. That is why our women are so slim."

I could say something about the porky teenagers I saw in Mr. Donut in Tokyo, but don't, to prove I can be culturally sensitive. I could tell her why I don't give a damn about my appearance right now. But my past is just that: mine. So I smile, wanting to say, "*So desu ne,*" that ubiquitous phrase of agreement, and to nod brightly like the ultra-chirpy female TV announcers do every time a male announcer opens his mouth. It reminds me of a wooden bird bobbing up and down into a glass of water: "*So desu ne*," in squeaky clean voices, over and over. I don't say it. Kawabata isn't stupid; she'd know I was yanking her chain.

We fill the awkward silences with menu discussions. "What do you eat in America?" "We eat many things." "Do you eat hot dogs? I had a hot dog once at Tokyo Disneyland." She must think food is my favourite topic.

After school, I coach Little Yasuko for her speech contest in September. Little Yasuko has short black braids, worn demurely above her shoulders, bangs to the eyebrows, round eyes, a wide smile. She is tiny, even for a sixteen-year-old girl, about four foot, ten inches, but she doesn't appear delicate: she's firmly rooted. Her pigtails and snub nose remind me of Anne of Green Gables, of whom she is passionately fond, along with the Chicago Bulls (Michael Jordan, especially) and the baby-faced actor from *Dead Poets' Society*.

"This is my dream," Little Yasuko begins, and I'm reminded of the Martin Luther King speech, which is in the English textbook. She wants to travel overseas and study to be a doctor.

She recites her speech and I tell her to focus on the audience, look the judges in the eye, and try to say "California" with diphthongs rather than all vowels pronounced. Then I ask if that really is her dream.

"Yes," she says, "but I think it is very difficult." In Japan, as I've already learned, this means impossible, as in Kawabata telling me, "I'm sorry, Miss Elaine-san, but it is very difficult for you to take *nenkyu* this month for a holiday." In other words, forget it.

"Dreams have another meaning, you know," I say, the schoolteacher in me rising up like koi, golden carp, surfacing for bread crumbs. "You dream at night. These dreams don't have to come true."

"What do you dream?" she asks. I frequently dream I'm back in high school to write a final exam, wandering the hallways of my old high school, a building similar to the one we're in now: three stories of grey cement built around a dirt courtyard.

"Too weird," she exclaims. I taught her this expression. She dreams about exams too, not passing them.

"I've had some weird dreams since I arrived in Japan. Must be the heat." I tell her about my experience, making it sound like a dream. But she turns serious.

"It is ghost. There are many ghosts in Japan. We are very old country, not like America. There are even *gaikako-jin* ghosts," she says, using the polite expression for "outside person." "We have ghost in Grandmother's room."

"Did your grandmother die recently?" I ask, worried about emotional repercussions from this conversation.

"Recently?"

Once I explain *recently*, she says, "No, no. Not recently." Little Yasuko likes to try out new words, taste them, roll them over on her tongue the way I'll savour sweet potato cakes from the Mito *omiyage* shop. "She didn't die recently. She live with us."

"Oh." Long pause as I try not to smile. "Why is there a ghost in her room?"

"It is *yurei*."

She explains that her grandmother is a widow, but before she was married she was in love with a young man whom Little Yasuko describes as "unsuitable."

"Her parents don't approve him," Little Yasuko says, her eyes shining, as if with unshed tears on her grandmother's behalf. "So she must marry Ojii-san, Grandfather. And lover is very unhappy. He die young. Forty-nine days after Ojii-san die, he show up. Grandmother know he is there because room is cold."

"Why did the ghost come back forty-nine days after your grandfather died?" I ask.

"Forty-nine days is when person goes to *anoyo*, other side," she explains. "So when Ojii- san left, my grandmother's lover returned."

"And was she happy to see him?" It's a bizarre question, but no stranger than the story.

"Yes, she is very happy. She miss him for long time. Now, she say, they like Heathcliff and Cathy. You know story?"

"You mean *Wuthering Heights?*"

"Yes, *Wu-ther-ing Heights*." She tries the title a few times. "*Wu-ther-ing Heights* is Grandmother's most favourite book. She say, is very Japanese book. I very much like."

"You've read *Wuthering Heights?*"

"Yes. But only in Japanese. In English, I think is *chotto muzukashi*." She tilts her head to one side and nods it forward as she says this, as if the expression must be softened and the phrase drawn out, a long stress on *chotto*.

"Yes, it's difficult. I read it in university. I thought Heathcliff was annoying." I thought he was an asshole, but I don't want to explain the word.

"But he is very brave. He keep trying, even though life is difficult. In Japan, we say *gambatte*. You know *gambatte?*"

"Persistent?" She looks puzzled, her brow furrowed beneath the bangs, so I search for synonyms. "To keep trying. He doesn't give up." I grab a pen and write *persistent* on a piece of paper, then wait for her to look it up in her dictionary.

"Yes, per-sis-tent. He does his best. And he never stop loving Cathy. Very sad. Very Japanese. He goes back for her after she die. That is true love, I think. Like Grandmother."

"Are there many ghosts in Japan?"

"Yes. Many, many people have died. And people who are unhappy in love, like Grandmother and her lover, they become ghosts. Maybe the ghost in your room was unhappy too."

Little Yasuko ends up convinced that there is a *gai-jin* ghost in my room. "It must be lonely," she concludes. "The only foreign ghost here. So it stay with you."

Loneliness I can understand. Is Little Yasuko lonely too? She has her parents, her grandmother, a younger sister in junior high. So why does she spend so much time talking to the fat *gai-jin* English teacher?

Saturday morning, I wake up and there's something in the corner again, a thin mist wisping up to the ceiling. I get up, go out into the kitchen to make a coffee, come back into the room, and it's still there. A vapour cloud in the corner, between the table and the futon cupboard.

"Good morning," I say, convinced that I am finally going mad, that loneliness is eating Swiss cheese holes in my brain. "*Ohayo gozaimasu,*" I add, just in case it's Japanese. It doesn't answer, thankfully. But it condenses. Instead of a misty-grey shape, all wavery around the edges, there's a grey shape of a man, complete with supernatural chill.

My ghost is dressed in a man's old-fashioned kimono of black and white, sashed around the middle like a dressing gown. He huddles in the corner, sheltering the left side of his face from my view.

"Who the hell are you?" I ask.

"Setsu? Is that you?" He sounds querulous, like a child just woken from a nap.

"Wrong number." Maybe he'll leave. I don't need a *gai-jin* ghost taking refuge in my bedroom.

"Setsu. Is my bath ready?"

"There's no Setsu here." This is beginning to remind me of those late-night phone calls I've been getting since the school gave out my phone number.

Me: *"Moshi, moshi."*

Student: "Har-ro (giggle)."

Me: "Hello. Who's this?"

Student: "Do you li-ku sex-u? (Giggle, giggle)." Click.

"Where am I?" the ghost asks. He sounds American, despite his Japanese attire. His hair is white and springs back from his forehead with a Mark Twain folksiness; he has sallow, wrinkled skin. If I had to attract a ghost, couldn't he be thirty-something and look like Laurence Fishburne. But this reminds me of Jeff and I turn my back to hide the tears.

"You are missing someone too," the ghost says. "With me, it was my mother. She was sent away when I was four. All my life I searched for her. Missing her, even after she died. Then I came to Japan. Like you." I turn around in time to see him vanish. I would say in a puff of smoke (the kind of expression I'd have to explain to Little Yasuko) but there is no smoke. He is just gone.

2. Running Away

My students excel at origami, the art of folding paper, *gami*, into shapes. During the lunch hour, they amuse themselves by creating intricate animals and designs. In English club, Little Yasuko tries to teach me how to fold a paper crane. The paper slips between my stubby fingers, while Yasuko effortlessly creates tiny birds in pink and gold.

She tells me the story of the young girl stricken with leukemia who vowed to make a thousand cranes or *tsuru*. "A thousand folded origami cranes make a wish come true," she says, her eyes wistful. "But girl dies at age of twelve. She only made 642 cranes."

At home, I sit cross-legged on the floor of my living room, labouriously folding squares of brightly patterned paper. Strings of origami cranes, in long folds of yellow, red, pink and green, dangle in the corner, a legacy of the last English teacher.

My *gai-jin* ghost materializes under the cranes, his black and white kimono looking more than ever like crumpled newspaper, and stares intently at me.

"What are you doing?" he asks.

I feign indifference, as if an elderly ghost in my living room is a common occurrence. "Making paper cranes."

He nods and says, "*So desu ne.*" Even his expressions are Japanese. He tells me he was one of the first foreigners to come to Japan.

"Like you, I am an American, although I was born in Greece to a Greek mother and a British father. My name is Lafcadio Hearn and I wrote many books about Japan."

"*So desu yo,*" I respond, mocking his serious tone.

"When I was twenty, I sailed to America to make my fortune. I almost starved," he muses. "I peddled mirrors door to door. In Japan, a mirror is known as the soul of a woman, but in America the mirrors reflected nothing but my own worthlessness. Later, I opened a restaurant called The Hard Times and fed the indigent."

"What made you come to Japan?"

"That," he says, "is a long story."

"So tell me. I had a lousy day at school and there's nothing on TV tonight." Nothing but Japanese game shows and CNN.

"Why does any foreigner come here?" he evades. "To get away. From home. From family. From failure. None of us are running to something. We are all running away." Huddling in the corner, he turns his head away so the left side of his face, the side with the milky-white blind eye, is hidden.

His bleak mood depresses me. I get up and leave the room. Slipping on my sandals, I grab my umbrella. I'll catch the 5:12 train to Mito, get a coffee. In San Francisco, I'd walk three blocks to the Starbucks. Only in Japan would I travel half an hour for a coffee.

On the train, I meet Kim and Maya, the sorority sisters. They're young and pretty with that chirpy cheerfulness, like small birds, twittering on about how great Japan is.

Kim isn't so cheerful today. She's complaining to Maya about her class. "So I'm in the classroom with Mishima-sensei, the Japanese teacher. The class stands up. She barks out *rei* and they bow in unison. Then she goes into this long-winded explanation, in Japanese, about the use of the passive. Can you believe it? These kids can't even answer a simple question like, 'What is your name?' in English, but they're learning the passive form."

"Well, they can be passive."

My joke goes right over Kim's head. She's ranting against her life: the long hours in the staff room of reading the paper, studying Japanese, breathing in second-hand smoke, and wondering what the hell she's doing here.

"Then we do this reading exercise, where I read the paragraph, but the kids repeat the words a half-beat off, so you get this ripple effect, like listening to three different music stations at the same freakin' time. And if I make a mistake, Mishima-sensei says, 'Kim-san, I think intonation is pronounced with stress on third syllable, yes?' Stupid cow."

While we're talking, a couple of my students sidle over to where we're standing, their skirts hiked up past the knees so that the blue and green Scottish plaid becomes a mini-skirt. The girls in my English club demonstrated the process for me last Friday, folding the waistband of the skirt over and over, and then cinching it with a belt. It makes them look like Sailor Moon, the crime fighting anime character with huge eyes, cute ponytails, and a schoolgirl uniform.

"Elaine-san. *Konnichi-wa.*"

"Hi." I don't remember their names. I have over five-hundred students, all dressed in the same uniform. I miss the costumes of home: Goth girls in black, the preppies in low-rise jeans, the gansta boys in hip-hop baggy pants. I know I'm missing subtle clues, signs of rebellion. My students are forbidden to dye their hair, pierce their ears, have part-time jobs. They do all three. Last week, a girl came to school with her hair dyed light brown and her home-room teacher made her kneel in the hall and then sprayed her head with black paint.

I introduce Kim and Maya, and Kim starts chatting in Japanese. The girls show wide-eyed astonishment at her proficiency. I'm sure I've acted just as surprised when someone from overseas speaks fluent English.

The students get off at Tomobe with smiles and waves for us.

"You're so lucky to teach senior high," Kim gushes. "The junior high kids are so young, you know. It's hard to have a conversation about anything with them."

"Yeah." Except for Little Yasuko, my longest conversations have been crank phone calls.

Mito station teems with commuters. I climb the steep stairs, puffing a bit. No escalators. I guess the disabled stay home. I want to stop halfway up to catch my breath, but the crowds push up from behind, while a stream of people flows down. At the top, I pause by a Poki juice machine, wheezing like a hurdy-gurdy as I try to catch my breath. The high-ceilinged station, which echoes like a giant bright cave, stretches out in all directions.

The sorority sisters invite me for a walk and Maya plays tour guide. "We'll go over to Lake Semba or Semba-cho. It's beautiful when the cherry blossoms are in bloom. The lake and the plum blossoms in Kairakuen Park are Mito's two claims to fame." She sounds like she's quoting *The Lonely Planet Guide to Japan.*

Kim adds her own bits of Japanese trivia. "Hiroshige Utagawa has some famous paintings of plum blossoms."

I have no clue who she is talking about.

She adds, "He's the *ukiyo-e* artist who influenced Van Gogh."

That, at least, is a name I recognize. The one who chopped off an ear.

"What's *ukiyo-e*?" I ask. I know they want to educate me, show me the beauty of Japan. I didn't come for the culture. I came for the cash. But I can't tell them that.

"*Ukiyo-e* are scenes of contemporary life. The artists also painted pictures of the floating world, the courtesans. But I prefer the scenes of nature." Kim is starting to sound Japanese. Next she'll be telling me, Japan is the only country with four seasons, and then describe the appropriate actions for each season. Maple leaf viewing in fall, snow and ice sculptures in winter, cherry blossoms in spring. I haven't figured out what we were supposed to do in summer. Melt, I guess.

Semba-cho may be known for its cherry blossoms, but now there are only leaves, heavy and green, drooping with the heat. We pass a couple of old men fishing on the banks of path lined with weeping willows. A pair of black swans with red beaks floats placidly near the edge of the yellow-gold grass.

Maya murmurs,

A pair of black swans
Mirrored in the flattened lake
Summer floating by.

"Is that a translation of a Japanese poet?" I ask. Maya, with her spiky hair and cat eye glasses, looks vaguely artsy.

She claims the poem as her own. "I've been writing haiku in English with my students. I guess I've got in the habit."

"We could all compose one," Kim suggests. "That's how haiku was originally done, as an opening poem for a group composition."

"What did you do, Kim, study nothing but Japanese culture at college?"

"University actually. UBC." I must look blank because she explains, "The University of British Columbia. I took a special course in Japanese literature and language. I went to a *ukiyo-e* exhibit at the Tokyo National Gallery last week with Simon. He brought a student along."

Maya lifts an eyebrow. "He's dating a student?"

"It isn't the big taboo it would be at home. The guys are in clover."

They start discussing the different English teachers they know, who's sleeping with whom. Looking over the shining surface of the lake, I watch the red sun set behind the hazy skyline of concrete rectangles dominated by the huge circle on the Daie department sign.

In San Francisco, it's six hours later. Midnight. The witching hour. For the past seven months, I haven't been able to sleep. I lie awake from midnight until two, reliving my life. I wonder if the girl who made the origami cranes did the same. Unable to sleep, she folded the tiny pieces of coloured paper, making the same wish with each precise fold. Let me live.

I think of the haiku I could write.

> *The sun slowly sets*
> *I am on the other side*
> *Yet nothing has changed*

Kim invites me to join them and a couple of friends for a drink at the Drunken Duck, a pub with a tipsy cartoon duck, holding a pint in one feathered hand, above the door. I introduce myself to Charlotte from somewhere in Alabama and Jules from Sydney, Australia. We're all English teachers, but the other two women work with language schools. I wouldn't be surprised if Charlotte is also a foreign missionary as she has that buttoned-up look. Jules is a thin woman with a strong Aussie accent who's been here five months.

"I came over in June and I thought I was gonna die. It rained for five weeks straight. Poured rain. You just can't believe it. And then it stopped raining and there was this great outcry in the papers. The rain has stopped. The rice crop is doomed. No worries, I thought, at least it's finally stopped raining."

Kim jumps in with her own experiences of rainy season. She lived here for a year, during university, so she outranks the rest of us. Even the *gai-jin* view people as *sempai* or *kohai*; you're ranked by number of months or years you've spent in Japan.

"My main problem is the language," I confess to Jules. "I don't speak a word."

"Have you heard about the lessons in Mito?" she asks. "This group of Japanese ladies gives lessons to foreigners. Five hundred yen a week, and bikkies at tea. You should come."

Jules and I leave at ten, so I can catch the last train south. A faint drizzle of rain falls and I open my umbrella, the black fabric liberally sprinkled with English, French, and German sentences, such as *however, is the people who make clothing manufacturing, conveyor belt industry sourced* and *les facteurs prinipaux consist dans ce qui fut un concours dipute.*

"Great umbrella," Jules says. "A wonderful example of Japlish. You know, English mixed with Japanese. It's like my ironing board. There's *fuck you* and *vagina* next to these *kawai* pink and blue teddy bears."

"*Kawai?*"

"*Kawai* means cute. The students, the girls at least, say it all the time. *Kawai so!*" She hits falsetto on the last word. Her sharp features already look familiar, like she's an old friend.

I ride the train home, surrounded by sake-soaked salarymen propped up on the seats. My ghost waits for me in the kitchen, an insubstantial grey form by the microwave.

"Why did you come to Japan, Elaine?" he asks.

"I was running away." I had a life in San Francisco, an apartment, a job, a fiancé. Then Jeff died and it all vanished, like mist burning off the bay. I flew to the other side of the world to escape. If I stay busy, if my world is completely different from what it once was, I can forget what I had and what I've lost.

"Why did you come to Japan?" I counter.

"After my restaurant failed, I reported the Tan Yard murders for the *Cincinnati Enquirer*. Yet I could not escape my bad fortune. My mother went mad after my father stole her sons from her. I never forgave him."

I think of my own parents. I haven't seen them in three years, since I told them about my relationship with Jeff.

"My fiancé was African-American," I say. "My parents wouldn't accept him. They didn't even come to his funeral. I haven't forgiven them."

Lafcadio nods slowly. "My first wife was mulatto. When our marriage was discovered, I lost my job at the Cincinnati paper. I tried living in New Orleans, the West Indies. Then, when I came to Japan, I finally belonged. I married Setsu, the daughter of an impoverished samurai, took her last name and became Koizumi Yakumo."

He doesn't mention what happened to his first wife. You can't look back when you're running away.

"You are dreaming your life, Elaine-san," he says meditatively. "*All beings are only dreaming in this fleeting world of unhappiness.* I wrote those words nearly one hundred years ago. I wrote many books, travelled to many places, loved many women. Now it seems as if it happened to someone else, to a character I created." He falls silent and then disappears, fading into the kitchen walls.

I can't look back. If I had a thousand origami cranes, I would wish for my old life, but now it's just a dream I once had.

3. Tasogare

Lafcadio materializes in the kitchen as I'm washing the dishes. I haven't seen him for a few weeks; I've been so busy at school. He's looking a little tatty around the edges, his black kimono even more worn, his hands fraying into grey shadows.

"Lafcadio. *Komban-wa.*" I show off a bit, hoping he'll realize that I'm trying to adapt. "*O-sashiburi desu ne.*" It's a long time since we've seen each other — it does have a certain ring in Japanese. He thinks I don't appreciate Japanese culture. "Where have you been?" I've missed him.

He traces a figure in the air, implying regions beyond my knowledge. Evasive, as usual.

"What are you doing?" he asks.

"Washing the dishes."

"Where are the servants?"

I wave a soapy hand around. "Do you see any servants?" Honestly, he has less idea of the work that goes into keeping house than any man I've met. Didn't he ever watch his wife do any housework?

"Why aren't you at school?" is his next question.

"It's Christmas vacation."

"Christmas!" Lafcadio exclaims. His face fades in and out of focus, the bones projecting forward like the Cheshire cat as it vanishes down to its smile. "What has Christmas to do with the Japanese?"

Good question. Fake candy cane decorations on the main streets and a few Santa Clauses scattered here and there are the only signs of the season. It would be better if there was nothing. No religious sentiment, no goodwill, no anticipation.

The only thing the same is the shopping. I sent a calligraphy scroll to my parents. A peace offering. I haven't phoned them since I arrived.

"It is your first Christmas alone. You should get out of the apartment," Laffy says. "Not stay at home brooding."

Does he read my mind or just my body language? It shocks me, how accurately he hits my sore spots. I want to yell, "Get out, get out of my apartment. You're dead, why are you lingering here, what the hell do you want?" But I don't. I want to know why he is here and Jeff isn't. If he leaves, I will be alone.

"Shall I tell you a story about mourning?" Laffy asks.

"Sure, as long as it doesn't interfere with my washing."

He settles himself in *seiza* in the corner of my kitchen, between the microwave stand and the fridge. Kneeling, he looks like a pile of old clothes in a heap. "This was published in my book *In Ghostly Japan*. Have you read it?"

"No." I tried to find his books on the sixth floor of the Kinokuniya bookstore, when I went down to Tokyo, but the selection ran more to kanji workbooks and Tom Clancy novels.

"This is a story from that collection. I discuss many of the different types of ghosts. In this story, the ghost arises from the smoke of a stick of burning incense, which carries with it a faint but never-to-be-forgotten scent, redolent of the back alleys and temples of Japan. There are many kinds of incense with diverse and beautiful names: *Tasogare*, which is Evening-Dusk or Gloaming in the poetic language, and *Wakakusa*, Plum-Flower, are two of my favourites. I have participated in incense parties, called *ko-kwai*, where guests gather to identity the different types of scents burned."

Lafcadio has a tendency to go off on tangents. Maybe that type of thinking endeared him in the circuitous ways of the east. I interrupt by asking if he has an actual story to tell.

"So impatient," he sighs. "This is a very old tale, from the Chinese, as are many Japanese classics, concerning the Chinese Emperor Wu. He lost his favorite concubine, the Lady Li, and great was his sorrow. One day, he determined to recall her spirit and, despite the anxieties of his counsellors, performed the rite of spirit recall. He lit the incense burner and meditated on the image of his beloved. In the wavering grey smoke, he perceived her form. Great was his joy as he looked again upon her beauty. But this was not enough for him. He reached out to touch her and, in an instant, the apparition vanished."

"What was the moral of that tale?" There is always a moral for Lafcadio. His mind is steeped in nineteenth-century British values, despite his attempts to escape, first to America and then to Japan. He reminds me of my British grandmother, with her fussy war-bride ways and endless nostalgia.

"Stories waver in the mind but when we attempt to hold them, they slip from our grasp," he admonishes.

"Ah so, little Grasshopper," I mock, but the cultural reference is lost, and he frowns in confusion. Obviously, Laffy hasn't spent his time in the afterlife watching TV. Just my luck to have a pedantic ghost in my kitchen.

"Any other stories," I ask, hoping to placate him, but he wavers and fades, just like the Lady Li. I've offended him.

"Come back," I call. "I was just kidding." No response. He comes and goes at will. "You can tell me some more stories. I'll listen more closely this time." He doesn't respond and the corner by the fridge remains empty. The refrigerator hums, the only sound.

"Okay, I'm out of here." I throw down the dish towel and bundle up in my winter coat, which is several years out of date and uncomfortably tight, and a striped scarf and mittens bought here. I wasn't expecting winter in Japan. Stupid of me. I yell, "I'm going to a movie in Mito," in case he's listening.

No snow, but it's colder inside than outside. I should insulate my windows. Every time there's a breeze, the faded curtains in the living room start swaying inwards, even though the windows are shut. The leaves of the English fern on my bookcase are brown at the edges.

At the train station, several of my students are waiting for the train. They're stuck with coming in to their club practice, even though it's Saturday and two days to Christmas. At least it was only for the morning.

"Hello, Miss Elaine." Kyoko, a third-year student, smiles and waves, but stays in her group of plaid-clad girls. Below the kilted skirts, their cold bare knees glow red. I've asked Little Yasuko if the girls aren't allowed to wear tights and she said they aren't fashionable. Teenage girls, the same everywhere.

I smile and wave back. Most of them will go as far north as Mito with me, but they'll keep their distance and so will I. It's the only way to function in their society where everyone sees you and knows what you're doing: keep your distance and be polite. It's not too bad in the short term.

Looking out the window, I see the suburbs of Mito, the blocky apartment buildings and swooping tile roofs of single-family homes flashing by.

Two hours later, I stumble out of a movie into the grey twilight, feeling just as depressed as when Laffy chased me out. A faint curtain of sleet falls; the street is crowded with open umbrellas.

I drift back down the hill to the station, sleet soaking the edges of my loafers, and then stop outside the windows of the Daie department store, wondering if I should get some ramen here or eat at home. Home. The word conjures up the apartment in San Francisco, a two-bedroom walk-up in a Victorian house. Wood floors. Cream ceilings with carved mouldings; a living room with a round stained-glass window of purple grapes and forest-green leaves; a gas fireplace: all of these compensated for a kitchen the size of a small closet and plumbing that shook the house every time we took a shower.

It hits me, the feeling of loss. I miss Jeff as intensely as in the first months, that blurred time last winter after he died. The ache pulls deep in my chest, like a settled cold that reaches down through the lungs. I start to shake, those recurring, uncontrollable deep shivers. Huddling in a corner of the recessed entrance to Daie, I grip myself with both arms, a tight wrestling hold to fight down emotion, widen my eyes so none of the tears falls. Well-dressed women and uniformed children come and go, staring at the *gai-jin* show. As if I care about loss of face. I'm a freak regardless.

I can't go back to my apartment in this state. From March to June last year, I'd come home from school, drop off my books and assignments, then head out, to a movie, a coffee shop, a restaurant, a concert, anywhere, so I didn't have to be in those echoing rooms with their nine-foot ceilings. Then Japan, the career change we'd planned together. His rejection letter arrived two weeks after the funeral, the same day as my acceptance. He had two years more teaching experience than me, but I can count the number of African-American teachers here on the fingers of one hand.

Across the street from the Daie is the store where I bought the calligraphy scroll. It should have incense. I pull myself back into organized fragments, walk a block down, climb the steps of the pedestrian crossway, and descend on the other side. A chime jingles as I enter.

Japanese dolls, gorgeously dressed and posed in the coffins of their glass boxes, line the left-hand wall. Huge rolls of red and gold kimono material are stacked to the ceiling at the back. A maze of chimes hangs in the small room, each cast-iron clanger weighted with a rectangle of paper bearing a kanji phrase for good fortune. Tiny statues of pigs roam everywhere, in white clay, glass, ceramic, dark wood, their red eyes staring at me, following me as I wind my way around the tables. On January 24, the year of the Pig begins.

I find the incense below the New Year's postcards: pyramid cones in packages of six, long sticks in fragrant paper envelopes. Picking two envelopes at random, I smell musk and the spicy odour of sandalwood. It reminds me of Ashbury, the hippies who linger — forty years after the Flower Power age ended — in dark, dingy shops, selling incense, drug paraphernalia, and tie-dye clothing. In contrast, this place has the clean, affluent feeling of an upscale Hallmark gift store.

Walking back along the street, I notice two life-sized goblins perched above the entrance of an office building, their spindly black arms holding a red banner over the door. I've never seen them before. The city is shifting around me. The goblins leer,

contorted grins and staring eyes, like the wicked faces that peer
from the corners of medieval buildings

"*Tadaima*," I call, opening the door to the apartment. The
word echoes. Laffy is still absent. It's so cold my breath hangs
in the air.

Setting up the incense stand on my *kotatsu*, I light one stick.
It takes me four tries to strike the match and the superstition
against that number, *shi*, with its association with death rises
in my mind. Nothing is without meaning here; even the simple
act of lighting an incense stick becomes a ritual. I'm doing it
all wrong. The incense blazes and I softly blow on it, reducing
the tip to grey ash. A thin line of smoke wavers up towards the
ceiling, divides in two, spiralling into loops, DNA strands. The
smell takes me back to when I was a teenager, spending nights
in my basement room, smoking pot and burning incense to
hide the bitter-sweet smell. Wind blows through the curtains. I
lean back, look at the smoke as it dances in the convex surface
of the TV, like two hands of a *maiko*, sleeves held back and
patterned fan waving, or the white and red ribbons that girls
use in rhythmic gymnastics. I focus on the dancing strands.

Nothing happens at first. "November Rain" by Guns N'
Roses plays in my mind: Axel Rose's screech of voice and the
ridiculous bleeding red roses from the video. Sleet turns to
rain outside my windows, the acrid smoke from the incense
rises and swirls, and I smell candles burning. The church in
San Diego, standing at the front with Jeff's parents. The open
coffin. I touch Jeff's hand, feeling a cold absence. Then blank
gaps of time. I remember singing "Amazing Grace" — his
parents wanted hymns — and hearing his brother's baritone.
He sounded like Jeff, singing in the shower. A revenant.

My parents didn't come to the funeral.

"We never met him, Elaine," my mother explained over the phone. "And you know we worried about you."

"Why the hell would you worry?" I whispered. Four of Jeff's friends from graduate school were in the living room and I didn't want them to hear me arguing.

"We just didn't see a future for the two of you. But let's not argue about it now. How are you feeling?"

"How am I feeling? My fiancé was killed in a hit and run two days ago."

"I didn't mean it that way. We're concerned, Elaine."

"If you were really concerned, you would come to the funeral." I didn't slam down the phone. I replaced it gently.

Jeff stares at me from the picture on the bookcase. "Let it go, Elaine," I hear him say. His voice had deep timbres that made the hair on my neck rise. The first time we slept together, he tangled my hair in his hands and gently pulled my head back so he could kiss my throat. "You are so beautiful," he whispered, and with him, I was beautiful, for the first time in my life.

I cut my hair when he died. There are no more mourning rituals in our culture, no need to wear black for a year, no going into seclusion. It would be easier if there were steps to follow, after the blurred week of the funeral, the friends dropping by with casseroles and halting expressions of sympathy. Jeff's parents drove up when I phoned that night. They took charge, leaving nothing for me to do. I stayed with friends. But after the funeral, I was on my own. This expectation in Western society: Once the body is buried, you should move on. Get over it. That story is finished.

Sometimes I think I've imagined Jeff, there is so little left to hold. Some pictures. A few books. His T-shirt that I sleep in, printed with a black and white caricature of Einstein. His voice in my mind.

A glowing tip of the incense stick falls off into a pile of ash, scatters over the shiny surface of the *kotatsu*. Lafcadio appears, a grey wisp of smoke rising above the tatami. "The stories we tell, Elaine. They drift in the air like the lingering scent of evening dusk. They are all that remains."

4. Baku

Kawabata-sensei slaps the *nenkyu* form for the English conference on my desk.

"It is in Tochigi. You must take the train," Kawabata snaps. She's annoyed with me because I made her fill her out the form. It's in Japanese, but she thinks that's no excuse.

I stamp it with my *hanko*, which looks like a thin tube of lipstick or a pinky finger. The *hanko* is the equivalent of a signature, stamped on everything from job applications to personal letters. Brides and grooms stamp their wedding certificate with a *hanko*.

"Remember, you must give a lecture on Sunday." Kawabata-sensei, the consummate teacher. Always ready with advice, whether I need it or not.

"*Hai*, Kawabunga," I whisper under my breath as she leaves.

"Miss Elaine-san," says Sumo-sensei, who sits at the next desk. "Did you wish something?" His name isn't really Sumo-sensei, but he watches sumo religiously and spent most of this month filling me in on the January tournament, one of four yearly tournaments. He is nearly retired and teaches only one or two classes a day.

"No, I was just talking to myself."

He nods, worried that the resident English teacher is going off her rocker. Later, he brings me a cup of *o-cha* and says, "*Kio tsukette, neh*. You must not work too hard." Since I've been doing the *Daily Yomiuri* crossword for the last hour, putting in time until my next class, I'm not sure how to interpret this comment. But I smile and hope he means well.

"I don't know what Kawabata's problem is," I complain to Jules that night at the Drunken Duck. Our Friday ritual, a drink and snacks at the Duck, then a pancake supper, *okonomiyake*, in a tiny restaurant two doors away. "She knows my Japanese is minimal."

"She's still pining for Sean."

"Sean, the wonder boy." I sip my sake. "Expert in all things Japanese."

"Even if he wasn't a wonder boy, she'd still prefer him. After all, he is male. Speaking of which," and Jules lowers her voice and looks around, "have you heard the latest gossip about a certain American male from your program?"

I check the room too. Two tall *gai-jin* men with beards are playing darts on the other side of the tiny L-shaped space. They must be researchers — the language schools don't allow teachers to have facial hair.

"Damn it, Jules, why do you always get the gossip before I do? What happened?"

"I heard that a teacher assaulted a junior high student in a 7-11." Her gravelly Australian voice pulls out the numbers, so that it sounds like "sieven a livin" and I see some burly white male pulling a tiny student through a sieve.

"Shit, no."

"Shit, yes. He was with a group of his friends, like-minded individuals you can be sure. He grabbed a girl's breasts and pushed her down. His friends pulled him off."

"Which one was it?" But I think I already know. He's an older man from Louisiana, balding and red-faced, as much of an outcast as I am among the smooth-skinned, young college graduates. He's the type who calls a woman "honey" while patting her ass.

"I don't want to name names," Jules says discreetly. "It's just a rumour. I didn't see it."

"Who did you hear it from?" How far does the *gai-jin* hotline extend?

"I heard it in Japanese class on Saturday."

There are hundreds of foreigners in Mito: some teach in language schools like GEOS and NOVA, as Jules does, and others work at the Hitachi research stations. A lot of people must know. I ponder my options. I could tell the local Coordinator for International Relations, our liaison with the Ministry of Education — Alain is an easy-going Frenchman in his late twenties, more mature than most of the people in the program. He'd know the proper procedures.

Or I could just let it slide. More and more, this is my inclination. Why be the nail that sticks up? I'm tired of being pounded down.

Jules goes over to pick up our seafood pizza. When she comes back to the table, I ask, "So how is work?"

Jules rolls her eyes. "Do you see what I'm wearing?"

She's in a knee-length dark skirt, white blouse, low heels. "What's different about it?"

"This is what I'll be wearing for the next five months. Orders from above. We have to dress *appropriately*. No long skirts, no jewelry. Flesh-coloured hose. Make-up."

I realize what's different about her. Her mouth is outlined in red lipstick. Her trademark gold hoops are missing.

She folds a piece of pizza, takes a bite. "A couple of people have quit. Remember Matthew? In my language class? Dark hair to his shoulders. They told him to cut his hair and he told them to fuck themselves. I think he has a job lined up in Tokyo."

"Are you going to stick it out?" I cross my fingers under the table. Without Jules, no more Friday night bitching sessions. No more adult conversations.

"I just smile, say '*Wakarimasu*' to my boss, and think 'Eat shit.' I might leave a month early, do some travelling."

"If you can hold on until March, I could take two weeks' *nenkyu* at the end of term."

"We could see Kyoto." Neither of us has been farther than Tokyo and we start making plans. Kinkaku-ji and Ginkaku-ji: The Golden and Silver Pavilions. The raked rock garden at Ryon-ji. The nightingale floors at Himeji-jo, the old Imperial Palace. Kyoto in cherry blossom season is a dream to get us through the next two months.

The next morning, packing for the conference, I realize I have a problem. When I flew to Japan, I was only allowed thirty pounds of luggage. The orientation book warned me that larger sizes of shoes wouldn't be available, but it didn't say anything about clothes. I've put on twenty pounds over the last two months, but I can't buy new clothes since every woman in Japan is supposed to be a size six or smaller. So I've been wearing Indian print wrap-around skirts with turtleneck sweaters to cover the bulging waistbands.

I stand in my white underwear, flipping through the hangers in my closet. My navy business suit doesn't fit; neither do my black wool pants. My shirts gape, my sweaters stretch revealingly over my chest, accentuating the substantial breasts of a matron. I've morphed into my mother, even though I'm only thirty. A middle-aged woman with no physical presence. Invisible, yet too much there.

Lafcadio appears in the corner. As usual, he is dressed in a man's black and grey kimono. Age sits well on him, bestowing a Yoda-like guise of wisdom to his shrivelled body, his yellowish-white hair.

"You didn't have this problem, did you," I accuse him.

"What problem is that, Elaine?"

"Nothing to wear."

"You have many Western clothes in your closet. Or you could wear Japanese kimono. I think nothing is more attractive than a graceful woman in a kimono."

"A graceful woman, yes. I'd look like a hippo in a muumuu." Sitting on my futon, I survey the closet with despair. I've always been the big girl, never model-thin or even pleasingly curvy. No, the word for me is fat and I've carried that label, a layer around the true me, the acceptable me, the pretty me. Until I met Jeff. I don't know why he could see past the extra pounds, but he could.

I'm weeping again. These past ten months, that's all it takes, one tiny setback and the tears flow. And no one to understand me but a *gai-jin* ghost, a hundred-year-old ghost, a ghost who loves Japan and everything it symbolizes. I haven't told Jules about Jeff's death. I'm afraid I'd start crying in the Drunken Duck and word would get around. *Did you hear about Elaine? She broke down in the Duck for no reason. She must be suffering from culture shock. Some people just can't handle life in Japan.* The *gai-jin* community feasts on rumours and innuendo.

"Elaine-san." Lafcadio stands up, a tiny, bent, ethereal man. I can see the corner of the desk behind his kimono sleeve.

"Don't weep. I can see Jeff's shadow, his *ihai*, protecting you. The beloved dead are always with us. It was so with my mother. It will be so with you."

But what does Lafcadio know of this despair? His is a nineteenth-century world, constructed on belief and fable. In Japan, he found a place that reflected his views, a place where you carry paper-white *bon* lanterns to light the way of the returning ghosts, a place where *butsuma* shrines draped with lotus blossoms and lit by incense honour the names of dead children, a place where love sometimes demands the ultimate sacrifice, *joshi* or mutual suicide.

What have I found? Reprieve. I'm haunted here, but it is a friendly haunting with no memories. Lafcadio, an obliging ghost, trails no pain into my room. In San Francisco, every corner I turned, every building, was haunted by Jeff. I kept seeing him on the bus, in our favourite corner at the Daily Grind, at bookstores, in the back rows of movie theatres. I'd walk into the apartment and it would feel as if he'd just been there, a breath of time separating us.

I miss air that tastes clean. I miss a world where I can read the signs around me. But I can't go back. I can't go forward. I'm stuck in one place, like those nightmares when I'm trying to run, and my feet won't move, I can't run, I can only wait for what slowly comes towards me. Lafcadio has told me the story of the Baku, the Japanese monster with the head of a lion, the body of a horse, and the feet of a tiger. It eats nightmares. I need the Baku to take away my fears.

I catch the train in the afternoon and stand swaying as the train clatters past rice fields, 7-11s, and houses, rice fields, 7-11s and houses. Oh my! I'm not in Kansas anymore, Toto. People quote that to me, once they discover I grew up in Abilene, Kansas, home of Mamie and Ike, that idealized couple from the fifties. The fifties — that's what Japan feels like to me. Salarymen in their sober business suits, housewives in their aprons. Polite children. Minimal violent crime.

'Do you have a gun?' ask my students, fed on the latest crime statistics in USA Today. The last time a boy asked me that, I went for an imaginary holster and he jumped a foot.

Most of the students get off at Mito and I take a seat. The sprawl of houses diminishes so I'm finally in *innaka*, the country. Staring out, I try to see what fascinated Laffy. It's so small, so flat. Of course, I have been dumped on the one flat plain of Japan, the great Kanto rice fields, stretching north and east from Tokyo. But there I go, comparing East and West again. As Laffy says, *The East has its own incomparable mysteries.* It's a quote from one of his books.

The station for Tochigi has a long line of concrete platforms flanking parallel sets of tracks, the green billboard strip with the station's name written in *hiragana* and English below the triangular roof. Jumping up, I grab my knapsack, rush for the doors as they slide open, jostling by men in suits. The men commandeer the last taxi and I'm left to walk to the hotel in the dusk.

Shouldering my pack, I trudge along the gravel edge of the road, dodging towards the ditch whenever a truck goes by, spraying me with dust. There's no demarcation point between the small village and the country, only a repeating procession of houses, convenience stores, fields, and vending machines. I trudge up a hill and then turn into the parking lot of a modern hotel, blazing with shining glass and electric lights. Tucked behind it is the old *ryokan*, wooden, low-eaved, dark with age. The two are grafted together, shiny new branches on an old trunk, or a new cumbersome shell grown while the old one is discarded to the side. Lafcadio would love the *ryokan*, the old, intimate, closed Japan, with paper *shoji* screens that conceal while they reveal; I prefer the modern version, which hopefully has showers.

I'm sharing a large tatami room with Kim and Maya. A framed *ukiyo-e* print hangs in the *takanawa* recess, above a stalk of white winter berries in a bamboo vase. *The Hanging Bridge of Clouds*. A wooden bridge reaches from the straw-roofed temple, tucked into the overhang of the cliffs on the far-right side, to a smaller temple set on a pillar of green, feathered with trees. Serpentine clouds billow, a second bridge arching back to the cliffs. A bridge of wood. A bridge of clouds. As we change for supper, Kim explains that the temple used to be in Tochigi.

"Where is it now?" I ask. She doesn't catch the joke.

"It's fallen into ruin, I imagine," she muses. "I'd like to have seen it. It's so ethereal." Turning her back, she pulls off her sweater and wriggles into a skin-tight red jersey.

I snort back a laugh. "Ethereal, my ass. I've heard temples and bridges weren't the only things those guys drew for *ukiyo-e* prints. Wasn't their other specialty women of the floating world? I bet the little temple on the left was for geisha." Lafcadio would like that.

"Actually, it was a tea house," Kim says. She points out details with her forefinger. "See how it's separated from the mainland. Look at the way the sweep of the cloud mirrors the movement of the bridge, joining the two sides. The tea house is part of nature, yet also separated. A retreat from the world, yet still part of it."

"All that trouble for tea. Now if it was sake, I could understand." Knotting the tie on my skirt, I'm reminded of my mother, how all of her clothes have a crêpey, middle-aged look.

When I return to the room after supper, the futons lie on the tatami like abandoned bodies. Kim and Maya have gone dancing. I stare at the tea house, wondering when I will feel part of the world again.

Sunday morning, I give a lecture on "Grammar in the Classroom." My colleagues listen attentively, though I'm sure none of them could identify a present participle. Most of them aren't teachers; they're language or business graduates who've come here to study Japanese or aikido or simply to take a year's break before they start work. I'm the anomaly, not them.

I corner Alain after the lecture. "I've heard some rumours are flying round."

"There are always rumours." He's a tall, craggy man with rumpled brown hair and an easy charm. Dressed in a navy suit, he looks like a Japanese salaryman, except for his confiding air. But he seems stiffer than usual, on guard.

"These concern a certain 7-11."

"I'm aware of the problem." He looks away and I wonder if anything will be done. Japan, land of evasions and half-answers. The conference doesn't end until tomorrow night, but my lecture is done. I don't have to stick around, pretending I'm having fun.

On my way home, the train stops at Tomobe. I move away from the door so that a crowd of suits can get off. As they jostle by me, one of the suits grabs my left breast and squeezes, hard.

I stand for a minute, shocked into immobility. Then yell, "What the hell do you think you're doing?" scrambling off the train after them as the doors close behind me with a whoosh. The men scuttle in a group for the exit, an anonymous shoal of blue backs.

"*Scabe*. Perverts." I scream after them. None of them turns around.

I stand on the edge of the platform as crowds brush by me, through the ticket turnstiles, out into the town. The train leaves the station, the high-pitched announcement reminding us, "*Kio tsukette. Abunai, dakara o-machi kudasai.*" Please be careful. Danger.

A group of junior high students peers curiously at me. "*Gai-jin da, gai-jin da,*" mutters one of the students under his breath.

"You can just go fuck yourself!" I'm past the point of cultural *détente*. They stare at me with horror. The monster *gai-jin* come to life. I eat small children. I stumble through the *shoji*-screen rules of Japan, trampling the Japanese way of life beneath my clumsy, size-nine feet. I am the Outsider who destroys everything she touches.

Back in my apartment, I pull off my sweater and unhook my bra. There is a reddening mark the size and colour of a squashed peach on the side and top of my breast. It will be a mottled purple and yellow by tomorrow. I bruise easily, the curse of fair skin.

Laffy appears, averting his eyes from my unclothed body.

"Elaine, you have been hurt." .

A hand reaching out. The sharp pressure, like catching my finger in a car door. The brutal intimacy.

I refasten my bra. My left side aches. "Some asshole grabbed my breast on the train. So much for Japanese politeness."

"Maybe he did not believe they were real."

"So he just reached out and grabbed!" I'm fed up with Laffy's defence of this country, with his cherry blossom view of everything Japanese. "What do you know? You never faced real life in this country. You don't know how they treat women. Is it okay to assault a teenager in a 7-11?" But that wasn't a Japanese man.

I dream that night of the Baku, the creature from Japanese mythology, with a horse's body and black and orange striped legs. Instead of a lion's head, it has a man's red face, surrounded by a mane. The Baku chases me through concrete tunnels, its hot breath burning against my neck. I stumble and it strikes, teeth sinking into my breast.

Waking, I breathe deeply until my heart stops pounding in my throat. I want Jeff's arms around me. That is what I miss most, since he died. Being held. Cherished. Protected.

5. Silence

The last day of February I wake up at four in the morning to rock music turned up loud. I go downstairs, thump on my neighbour's door, but he won't open up, or else someone else beat me to it and killed him. Wish it had been me. That's the third time in two weeks. Another complaint for Kawabata-sensei, not that she does anything. Last Tuesday, the gas cut off in the middle of the night and I woke up to no heat and no hot water.

"Try having an ice-cold shower in a freezing apartment and then smiling for your class," I tell Lafcadio. "It can't be done."

"Try living in Kumamoto for a year," he replies. "A horrible place, no heat at all and no showers."

"Yes, but you had Setsu to draw your bath every night."

There is no reply and he sulks in the corner. Sometimes I think Lafcadio came all the way to Japan to find a woman who would put up with him. Are the women more tolerant? Or do cultural differences mask the usual petty problems that destroy relationships? Jeff and I fought over words. He called me *baby*. "Come over here, baby." I hated it. It made me feel about two feet tall. He complained that I didn't use pet nicknames at all, not lover, or honey, or sweetie. I felt silly saying those words.

"What did you call your wife?" I ask Laffy.

"I called her Setsu," he says. "Or *oku-san*."

"*Oku-san?*"

"It means wife, Elaine-san. You should study your Japanese more carefully."

"I meant as a pet name." I ignore the complaints about my lack of Japanese. Why would I need to know the word for *wife*?

"A pet name. I do not understand. Do you mean like a dog or a cat?"

"What did you call her when you felt affectionate towards her?" I'm tempted to say, "when you had sex," but I don't want the details of Laffy's sex life.

"Once our son was born, I called her *haha*." Mother. *Ha ha.* Charming. He thinks he is being helpful. If *wife* and *mother* are the only terms of endearment in Japan, I pity the women. *Baby* now sounds wonderful. Cherished. I shouldn't have complained. But I didn't know, I didn't know that things wouldn't last. That they were temporary gifts.

Sitting at the kitchen table, I cradle a cup of tea between my palms, the *kotatsu* quilt draped over my shoulders for warmth. I'll be puffy-eyed and short-tempered in class again. Short-tempered. Why short? Why not small-tempered? One of those English conundrums that Kawabata-sensei likes to bring to my attention. "Elaine-san, why does the pot call the kettle black? What is the last straw?" I want to quiz her about why Japanese has so many counting numbers: *hitotsu, futatsu* for age; *hitori, futari* for people; *ippon, ni-pon* for long, thin items like pencils and beer bottles; *ichi-mai, ni-mai* for flat items like cards. Everything must be properly categorized, put in its place. *Ichi-gai-jin, ni-gai-jin, san-gai-jin.*

I see the students who don't fit in and wonder what happens to them. The boy with epilepsy, who had a spell a few weeks ago in my class. The overweight girls. The half child.

Kawabata-sensei whispered the description to me one day as we were walking back to the staff room after class, asking if I'd noticed him. Of course I had, he's tall with lovely cheekbones.

His mother is Swedish. "He is half," she said. I wonder where he fits in Japan. Nowhere. Not *Nihon-jin*. Not *gai-jin*. *Nowhere-jin*. In the staff room, I am *nowhere-jin*. It's one big room, divided into three sections for first-year, second-year, and third-year homeroom teachers. The vice-principal sits at the front, chain-smoking furiously, running the show like vice-principals everywhere while the principal sits downstairs in his fancy office and drinks *o-cha*. Every morning we stand and bow, either to the vice-principal or the flag that hangs over his desk. I sit in a corner next to the filing cabinets, isolated from the bustle around me. My desk is bare, except for a row of teaching manuals and English videos, a stark contrast to the clutter of books and papers stacked high around me.

At lunch, Kawabata-sensei strides over, drops a page of paper on my desk. "Please correct Miss Yasuko Tanazaki's speech. She will be in a speech contest in Mito next month." She marches away, her back stiff as a ramrod.

A Letter from My Friend

I owe what I am to my friends. I'd like to talk about what I learned through my friendship with a friend of my junior high school days.

In October, we have a music festival. We want to win the contest at any cost as the last memory. However, our class would not unite in practicing. Some classmates weren't serious about the practise. They sometimes wanted to go home right after school. I thought everyone in my class should cooperate each other. I made them stay in the classroom as a leader.

When the results of the contest were announced, my heart was beating. I hoped we would win the contest because everyone did their best on the stage. "The first prize is class 3-1." "Thank you for your cooperation," I shouted to my classmates. I was very satisfied at result.

Several days passed since the music festival was over. One day I noticed that my friends had become unfriendly to me. Why were they were unwilling to talk to me? I couldn't find the reason.

Next day, one of my friends gave me a letter. The letter was great shock to me. The letter said that I had become pushy. It gave me an advice that you should be tolerant to your classmates. How was I pushy? Without my effort, my class wouldn't have gotten the first prize. All the students should have expressed their thanks to me.

The letter showed me another myself. It was unbearably painful to look at the other side of me. Tears were running down my face. I shut myself up in my room. "Am I too pushy?" I said to myself again and again. I was afraid my friends would forsake me forever. I must have hurt my classmates without knowing it. I have to change my attitude toward them. I have to be considerate of them.

The letter was my friend's kindness for me. Now I think I could change myself a little better. Now I have good friends.

Yasuko Tanazaki

The other side of me. Little Yasuko seems like the other side of me, the side I would be if I'd been born in Japan. The strong female to be hammered down. Since the man grabbed my breast on the train, I've seen danger everywhere. I wish it were just *gai-jin* who are subject to such attacks, but I know better. A man wrote a manual for groping women on Tokyo subways: he was at 1000 women and counting. My friend, Jules, heard about a flasher who was targeting kindergarten children. I'm lost in the maze of Japan.

The Eater of Dreams

I return Little Yasuko's corrected essay at English club. English club has six regular students, all girls, so I can't discuss the essay immediately. In the audio-visual room, we watch half of *The Little Mermaid*, one of several children's videos a friend sent over. The mermaid has given up her voice, traded her tail for legs. In the Disney version, unlike the Hans Christian Andersen fable, the mermaid doesn't suffer agonizing pain, like walking on glass, with each step in the strange new world.

While the other girls are filling out a questionnaire about the movie (*What does the sea witch take from Ariel? Who helps her to swim to the surface?*) I hand back Little Yasuko's essay.

"This is very good."

"Thank you. I will do my best at the contest."

"*Gambatte.*"

She smiles. I recognize that teacher's smile. Kawabata-sensei smiles the same way when I finally remember some expression she's taught me five times. I smile when one of my students puts up his or her hand in class and answers a question, even if the answer is wrong.

"How did you feel when you won at the music festival?" I ask.

"I felt very happy," she says. "But then, not so happy after."

"But would you have won if you hadn't encouraged your classmates to practise?"

She shakes her head emphatically, a gesture I taught her. The Japanese equivalent is waving your hand rapidly in front of your face, a habit I've picked up when denying I speak Japanese: "*Ie, mada mada jozu ja arimasen*" while waving my hand in front of my eyes like windshield wipers swishing in a heavy rain.

"No," she says. "But it is more important to have my friends."

"We have an expression in English," I say. "You can't please everyone. That means that there are things you have to do that won't make other people happy. But it is more important that you do these things, even if other people aren't happy. I think you were right to encourage your classmates to do their best."

Little Yasuko frowns, a sign that she's listening carefully. But I'm not sure she hears me. Even while I'm speaking, I know I can't counter-balance sixteen years of cultural training. I don't even know that I should. Who am I to say I'm right? Maybe friends are more important than excellence, good feelings within the community more important than individual initiative. She has to live here. I don't.

The next day is March 1. Graduation Day. When I walk into my chilly kitchen, Laffy is huddling in the corner. I open my mouth to say "Good morning" and nothing happens. Not a croak, not a squeak. Total silence.

"Elaine-san," Laffy says. He must be concerned to add the *san*; he's usually not that formal with me. "What is wrong?"

Clearing my throat, I try again. Nothing. No voice. I feel as if I've suddenly been turned off or transported to a land of silent movie pictures. Japan has done its best to silence me and has finally succeeded. No pain, only an unpleasant rawness at the base of my throat. I've been drinking hot tea all week, cursing the raw weather, the constant rain.

"Are you ill?"

I must look laughable, opening and closing my mouth like a fish, no sound coming out. I point to my throat.

"Your throat. That is most serious. You should see a doctor."

I shake my head. I've heard about Japanese doctors from Jules. She had pneumonia in December, so she went to a doctor in Mito. He didn't even listen to her chest, just prescribed a regimen of pills, red pills, blue pills, yellow pills. After feeling like her head was sunk in sand for a day, she went off the pills, stayed home for three days with the heat turned high, and drank fluids until, as she said, "I was floating away in pee." No Japanese doctors for me.

Maybe a cup of tea with honey will soften up the vocal cords. And a hot shower. I try both remedies, but even after three cups of tea, my voice is still absent. I'd call in sick, there's not much point in teaching with no voice, but I can't use the phone.

Riding to school, I realize I'm sicker than I thought. I'm panting and sweating both. The students surge by me on their black one-speed bikes, smiling and waving, "Good morning, Miss Elaine-san." Nodding, I concentrate on pushing one foot after another. I'm shaking by the time I reach school, just a fifteen-minute ride, and also late.

First, I go into the bathroom to wash my face and comb my hair. I'm wearing the blazer of my navy suit in honour of graduation, but I look rumpled and messy, the white blouse damp around the collar. Flushed cheeks with puffy eyes above them. I look like I've been on a bender. Running water over the comb, I coax my fly-away hair into sedate lines. Then into the staff room. Kawabata-sensei grabs me as soon as I cross the threshold.

"Elaine, you missed the morning meeting."

I open my mouth, nothing comes out. God, what if this is permanent, if my voice never comes back? I can't teach without a voice. Gesturing wildly, I point at my throat. I feel like the Little Mermaid, stranded on dry land and unable to communicate.

"What is the problem?"

Is that concern in her voice? Finally, I think to grab a pencil and some paper. *I have lost my voice*, I write.

"Why didn't you tell me you were ill?" she says.

How does she think I could inform her? By telepathy? There is no need to bite my tongue today, as my sarcastic remarks are pre-silenced.

"You must stay for the graduation ceremony, but then you should go home to rest. *Kio tsukette neh*. Please take care of yourself." She actually pats my shoulder. She's wearing a pink kimono in honour of graduation. This is a side to Kawabata I've never seen.

At least the staff room is warm, although my desk is far away from the stove. Normally, at this time, I check over my lesson plans for the day, read the *Daily Yomiuri*, have a cup of tea with Sumo-sensei. He's absent today, probably helping set up the gym.

The gym is freezing, an open icebox. I take one of the chairs on the side, pitying the students who must sit on the bare floor, the girls in their skirts, rows and rows of plaid, like dolls on a shelf. Except for the lack of chairs, it is like a gym at home. The ceremony is the same too, boring speeches, presentations. No parents. No party.

Last year, in San Francisco, my students wore thousand-dollar dresses to grad. The year before, Jeff and I were chaperones. Students giggled as we waltzed sedately by.

On the way back to the staff room, I peer out the window. Soft wet flakes of snow fall gently, like cherry blossoms, melting instantly into puddles on the cement in the central courtyard. Lines of black bicycles shelter under sheds on the fourth side of the courtyard; the modified Y of the school wings forms the other three sides. Students under multicoloured umbrellas snap each others' pictures in the snow.

The snow switches to sleet as I ride home, huge wet splats pelting down on my jacket, my skirt, soaking through to my skin, plastering my hair to my head in limp strands. I park the bicycle at the bottom of the stairs, stagger up the steep steps, and let myself into my cold apartment. Peeling off my clothes in the bedroom, I run a hot bath and soak in my tiny tub, dry off with the towel that is still damp from this morning's shower. My last batch of laundry is strung out on the plastic clothes rack, both damp and stiff. Swathed in a grey flannel nightgown, I curl up under a pile of blankets and fall asleep.

At four, I hear the tinkly sounds of Edelweiss. Shadows in my bedroom. I drift in and out. A shape rises in the corner of the bedroom, forms, dissipates. I feel Jeff sitting beside me on the bed, his hand on my forehead. "Shh. Go back to sleep." His hand is large and warm.

In the morning there's a burning sensation on my left side and back. My throat aches, a flypaper scratch. I'm feverish. They will know I'm sick. I can't phone. I pour a glass of orange juice, take two aspirin, and crawl back into bed.

Wake up in the afternoon. Sunlight bleaches the curtains for the first time in a week. I'm drenched with sweat, the flannel nightgown twisted around my body like a winding cloth. My back feels like someone pressed an iron on it. I have to get out of the nightgown and change the sheets. Stumbling around, I pull the sheets from the futon, dump them in a heap in the corner, and remake the bed. I sit down for a moment to regain my strength and suddenly I'm in my old apartment, the two places overlaid like a double exposure.

Jeff and I, waltzing in the bedroom. My head nestled against his chest, listening to his heart beat. Thump, thump, thump. The bedroom swims back into focus, my bedroom in Japan, the futon on the tatami floor, a heap of clothes in the corner. Laffy? No, it's the dirty sheets.

I go into the bathroom to take a shower. As I pull the flannel nightgown over my head, I see a constellation of red marks on my left side. Craning my head over my shoulder, I see a large mark on my back. Flea bites? I haven't been diligent about putting out my futon every morning to air it out. But flea bites are supposed to itch, not burn.

The bathroom wavers back and forth. I sit on the yellow plastic stool to shower, bracing myself with a hand against the wall. As I'm drying off, I forget about the marks, briskly rub the towel against my back, and gasp with pain.

The bedroom. I doze and then wake. Something in the corner. Is Laffy there? No, he has deserted me. Everyone has deserted me. Jeff has deserted me.

Dark again. Edelweiss plays. I'm rocking back and forth, weeping, weeping. My head aches, my back burns. What day is it? Graduation was two days ago. March 1. It's March 3. The one-year anniversary.

I'm at home and the phone rings. The hospital. Come down immediately. There's been an accident. Jeff had been riding home on his bicycle. Hit and run.

Killed instantly.

It's so dark. I'm in a heap on the floor. I hear Jeff's voice, soothing as liquid honey. "It's all right, Elaine." He's holding me close, hugging me, our bodies a perfect fit, spooned along our entire length, back, legs, warmth all through me. "It's all right. Hush, baby."

It's light. I hear pounding. The door. Sitting on the edge of the futon, I pull on my track pants. My back is on fire, but my mind feels clearer. I must have sweated out the fever. Four o'clock in the afternoon. I've lost a day. Like when I flew to Japan. One day, gone.

Kawabata-sensei is at the door. "Elaine-san. You weren't in school again today. Are you still ill?"

Isn't it obvious? I nod.

"Get dressed. I will take you to the doctor. Bring your orange health card."

I want to protest, but the rash has me scared. I feel as if I've walked through fire, a handprint of pain on my back, my left side. I must have been delirious last night. Jeff was here.

I pull on jeans and a T-shirt. No bra. I try to fasten one but can't stand anything touching my left side. Digging through my official papers, I find the health card and then walk down the stairs slowly, feeling fuzzy and weak. As I sit down in Kawabata's Honda, my back connects with the seat and I gasp and sit forward, hunched over with pain. We drive into town.

In the office, after we've waited for half an hour, we're admitted. Kawabata-sensei comes in with me, confers with the doctor. I catch the words for fever, *netsu ga arimasu*, and sore throat, *nodo ga itai*.

I've brought my dictionary with the handy list of words for medical conditions. Gesturing to Kawabata, I point out the word for dull pain, *nibui itami*, and pat my left shoulder. The doctor nods and motions for me to pull up my shirt, looks carefully but doesn't touch. Am I infectious? Maybe I'm dying, some horrible skin condition like leprosy or flesh-eating disease. My limbs will fall off. I'll rot from the inside out.

Kawabata translates. "He says you have *mizuboosoo*." She looks the word up in her dictionary. "Chicken pox."

Shaking my head, I write, "I've had it before."

"He says, it is a kind of chicken pox you have after you've had chicken pox the first time. I do not know the word in English." The doctor launches into a long explanation. Kawabata nods respectfully, occasionally interjecting, "*So desu ka.*"

"He says if you get very tired, sometimes chicken pox comes back. It is good you came in. He can give you pills for the infection; it will heal in a few weeks."

I write, "I've been run down." She looks at the words. "Run down? Like a car?" I write, "An expression for very tired." She nods, "*So desu.* Run down. Very good. Thank you, Elaine-san." Shaking my head, I write, "Thank you very much." She smiles and laugh lines appear, making her look years younger. I bow deeply to her and the doctor.

I'm given blue pills, red pills. I take them gladly. Kawabata-sensei buys me orange juice and cups of instant chicken soup on the way home.

"Don't worry about school," she says, as she drops me off at the apartment. "I will fill out your *nenkyu* forms for Thursday and Friday." The *sempai-kohai* relationship is finally working for me. I shouldn't have been so independent.

The Eater of Dreams

Sitting at my kitchen table, I drink a cup of hot chicken soup. The red pills must have codeine in them, I'm floating away.

6. The Eater of Dreams

"*Tadaima.*"

Friday evening and the school term is over. I'm free for two weeks. I finish supper, telling Lafcadio about my week. He sits by the *kotatsu*, his head turned so the milky-white blind eye is hidden.

"Sunday, before I leave to go to Kyoto with Jules, I'm going to Kawabata-sensei's house. She invited me to a tea ceremony. She's going to dress me up in one of her kimonos."

"She has invited you to a tea ceremony? That is a great honour. I myself have participated in many tea ceremonies."

"Great, you can fill me in on all the gory details. Just let me do my own ritual first."

I fill the metal kettle with water, turn on the gas and put the kettle on to heat, then take down my teapot and a china cup, the one with a handle and a design of blue cranes flying over a cone-shaped mountain. Earl Grey is the only variety of packaged tea available in the foreign store in Mito, but it's a change from *o-cha* and Lipton. I swirl hot water in the teapot, as my English grandmother taught me, and then add two teabags and wait four minutes. Fortified with a cup of tea, with generous dollops of milk and sugar, I ask Laffy, "So what happens in this tea ceremony?" I have a vague notion of wooden tea houses in deep-green, mossy gardens (an image from the movie *Shogun*) and rows of serious kimono-clad ladies, delicately sipping. "Do I have to raise my pinky finger? Do I put the milk in first?"

"Tea is a very important ceremony," Laffy instructs. "You must act like a proper Japanese lady."

He spends twenty minutes instructing me in the art of tea. "You must not make faces when you see the tea. It is not English tea. It is green, almost spinach-green, and will taste bitter and be whisked to a foam like ocean spray."

"Why drink it if it tastes bitter?"

"You must not ask questions. Just open your eyes and mind and surrender to the serenity of the ceremony. A form of meditation."

"Right. The zen of tea." I'm teasing him, something Laffy usually accepts with bad grace. Now, though, he is not paying attention to me, lost in his own world.

"I once wrote a story about tea, from the fragment of an old Japanese tale. A man sees the face of a young samurai in his cup of tea. He empties the cup, washes it, fills it again, and again sees the face, mocking him. The samurai's mocking smile enrages him and he drinks, realizing only after it is too late that he has swallowed a soul."

"Another one of your creepy stories. What happens next?"

"There is no ending to this story and I did not invent one. I leave it to you to imagine the consequences of swallowing a soul."

Being dressed up as a *gai-jin* doll has its advantages. Where else would I get to wear a silk spring kimono, decorated with pale pink and red plum blossoms on a white background? Kawabata-sensei has me strip me down to my underwear.

"Elaine-san, what are these marks on your back?"

Perhaps she imagines I've indulged in some ritual Christian purification for Easter. I tell her they are scars from my bout of chicken pox in March. I've since learned that it wasn't actually chicken pox, it was shingles or, more technically, herpes zoster, a disease that sounds suspiciously like an STI. The scars no longer hurt and they're fading slowly, but there is still a red blob the size of a palm on my back and a cluster of dots under my arm. They look like arrows or cranes flying, if I turn my head sideways. The other scars from that time are hidden. Did Jeff return that night I was delirious? His presence is no harder to believe than Lafcadio's. How many people in Japan have one-hundred-year-old ghosts in their apartments? How many people are visited by dead lovers?

Kawabata-sensei wraps me up, first in a white long blouse without buttons; then the kimono itself, folded left over right, the sleeves long and square, the collar scooping away to reveal the neck; then the *obi*, a stiff red sash that surrounds me like a chastity belt, holding me in so tightly I have to take quick, shallow breaths. My chest sticks out above it like that of a matron in a firm corset. She secures the *obi* over a large block of material with a red iris embroidered on it, and then knots a white cord around the *obi*. I'm feeling more and more like a brightly wrapped package: Western *omiyage*, wrapped and wrapped again in the Japanese way. On my feet are the split-toed white socks called *tabi*, usually worn with *waraji*, a sandal made of rice-straw. Thus adorned, I make my way downstairs in short, short steps, walking as carefully as a pregnant woman trying not to trip.

The ladies who come to tea all sigh and wave their hands, like a field of rice bowing in the breeze. I am the guest of honour. I kneel and bow, almost knocking my head against the floor, before entering the tea chamber. The tatami flooring is bare, no furniture at all. Rather than plain *shoji* screens, the walls are ornamented with sprays of pale pink and white flowers. In the raised *toko-noma*, a wooden dais at the far end of the room, is the flower arrangement, which looks bare to me: a single stalk of flowering cherry in a vase shaped like a tube of bamboo. Above it hangs a scroll with a verse in kanji dripping down its length, black smears of ink.

Kawabata-sensei explains. "The scroll expresses a feeling for the season. The poem is one of Ono no Komachi's. It translates roughly as *The flowers fade too swiftly / So too does my body / As the rain falls endlessly.* When we see the flowering blossoms, we are reminded of their short lives and our own short lives."

"Life is transient," I say. "As Shakespeare says in *Macbeth*: *Life's but a walking shadow, a poor player / That struts and frets his hour upon the stage / And then is heard no more.*"

"Ahh, *so desu ka*." I hope I've impressed her. Sometimes I feel so uncultured here, a piece of grit that needs layers and layers of oyster spit before I'll glow in pearly splendour.

I'm introduced to the six other ladies, all in plain rich kimonos of dark green, crimson, pale amethyst, grey-blue, silvery-grey, and bronze, whose names slide by my ears in liquid consonants. I smile and bow, then try to arrange myself as gracefully as my companions, but the kimono bunches under my feet and gaps as I carefully lower myself to my knees. My knees begin to ache immediately as I fold myself into *seiza* position, with my feet tucked under my ass.

The tea lady, in a pale kimono patterned with a delicate grey landscape, is an expert. A section of tatami has been lifted out, revealing a small area for boiling the water. An iron pot holds the water, which the tea lady gently ladles out with a bamboo scoop into the tea bowl, then adds the powdered green tea and whisks it. As the bowl goes around the half-circle, each lady rotates the bowl, admiring the green of the tea against the bowl's rough rim of mottled orange and the glazed gold interior, and then takes a sip and wipes the edge with a *fukusa*, a square cloth of royal purple. The colours of the kimonos glow in rich jewel hues against the white walls.

When the tea bowl comes to me, I smile and take it carefully, concentrating. I don't want to spill anything on the kimono. I look down and see green foam, thick as paint. And something else. Lafcadio's wrinkled face, one eye smiling, the milky eye obscured by his white hair.

I look up, startled. Kawabata-sensei murmurs encouragingly, "Just take a small sip, Elaine. It is bitter, but it does not taste so bad."

Looking down again, I see Lafcadio's face is still there, framed on all sides by foamy green.

"What are you doing here?" I whisper harshly.

I sense unease on either side. I'm disturbing the serene peace of the ceremony. Grimacing at Laffy, I set my lips to the edge of the bowl, take one small sip. He winks at me and disappears. I pass the bowl to the lady on my left.

The tea bowl has gone around the circle; the utensils have been washed. My knees are screaming for release and my feet are numb. Once the obligatory photo has been taken, I carefully slide my feet out and to the side.

The lady to my right smiles as I slump over towards her. She murmurs something and I catch the words *seiza* and *muzukashi*, the expression for difficult which I hear every time I give one of my classes a pop quiz.

"*Hai, muzukashi*," I nod.

"*Ohh, jozu desu.*" The standard Japanese politeness, complimenting me on my nonexistent language skills. She then speaks with the lady on her right and they smile and nod.

Kawabata-sensei leans over. "She says that you are very tall. Japanese people are short because we spend so much time kneeling. It shortens the legs."

That's a different explanation. I always thought it was genetics and the diet which, until thirty years ago, was high in rice and fish, low in red meat and dairy products. Certainly, some of my grade eleven boys are my height, five foot, eight, or taller. Maybe they don't kneel much.

"My father is tall," I explain. The struggle to translate. "*Watashi no otoo-san wa . . .* " What the heck is the word for tall? *Ooki!* "*Ooki desu.*" Actually, *ooki* might just mean big, but what the hell, last time I saw him, Dad needed to lose some weight.

"*Ahh, so desu ka.*" We have achieved cross-cultural communication. Fortunately, we can stop, as the tea ceremony is finally over. I stagger to my feet, an awkward giraffe unfolding my limbs, to a chorus of polite giggles. Kawabata-sensei takes my elbow, probably worried that I'm about to crash through her fragile *shoji* walls.

"Now we will have lunch," she announces. She goes into the kitchen and ties a lacy white apron around her kimono. I follow her so I don't have to sit down again. I'm feeling a bit odd, light-headed. What was Lafcadio doing in my tea bowl? Is my subconscious playing tricks? I've never seen him outside my apartment before.

Returning home, an hour later, I call, "*Shitsurei shimasu*" as I open the door and slip off my shoes. No response. I check the bedroom, the kitchen, calling "Laffy, are you here?" but he doesn't answer, doesn't appear. This is nothing new as he often vanishes for days at a time. Typical man. He shows up when he wants, disappears for days. I have no telephone number for the other side. I don't know what he does there. I still don't know why he's here, in my apartment.

Jules and I leave Monday morning for Tokyo. After a day of shopping and a movie, we catch the overnight bus to Kyoto, leaving at eleven from a bus terminal that looks like bus terminals everywhere: blue and orange plastic chairs in the waiting room, scruffy backpackers waiting outside under the neon glow of bright lights. The bus itself is surprisingly luxurious; the seats recline and we're provided with pillows and blankets.

We settle in for a good chat. I tell her about the tea ceremony, leaving out Lafcadio's surprise appearance.

Jules falls asleep around two. I am staring out the window, marvelling at the utter blackness of the night, when I hear a voice.

"Elaine, thank you for taking me to Kyoto." It is Laffy.

"Where are you?" I whisper.

"I am with you. I am now a part of you." This is sufficiently mystical to creep me out, until he starts making demands.

"Do you think it would be possible to see Kinkaku-ji and Ginkaku-ji. And the cherry blossoms along the Path of Philosophy? And Heian Shrine? The *tori* gate outside the shrine almost reminds me of Itsukushima shrine, rising from the tranquil blue waters of Hiroshima Bay. I have written a fascinating sketch of my travel experiences there."

"Do you have any other requests?" I ask, hoping no one can hear me.

"If only you could travel as far as Matsue, so that I could see my house one more time. But that would be difficult."

Jules and I walk the winding streets of Kyoto, accompanied by an invisible tour guide, murmuring comments in my inner ear. At Kinkaku-ji, the Golden Temple, burnt down in 1956 by a mad monk and completely rebuilt and reguilded by subscriptions from the Japanese people, he marvels, "It is exactly the same as before. This is most astonishing." Ryoan-ji, with its raked garden of white gravel and fifteen rocks. I sit on the raised wooden balcony along one side of the garden, with Lafcadio admonishing me: "Look carefully, Elaine. If you open your inner mind, the rocks become the islands and the white gravel is the sea lapping at the bosom of Japan."

At the youth hostel, he discreetly vanishes and Jules and I can bask in peace in the women's *onsen*, the steaming water sloshing against our bodies. I start giggling at the sight of my breasts and knees rising out of the water like islands and suddenly I'm crying, and Jules is asking, "Are you okay, Elaine?" and I can't explain what's wrong.

The next morning, the cherry trees nestle against the striking orange walls of Heian Shrine; the trees in the inner courtyard blossom with white paper prayers. "Elaine, could you tie a prayer to the tree for me?" I purify my hands with icy water from the fountain at the base of a granite dragon statue, before writing a prayer. I use one of Lafcadio's epigraphs, an old Japanese love song — *Mijika-yo ya! Baku no yume ku, Hima mo nashi!* — and tie it on a branch in the cluster of trees below the row of iron lanterns and swooping green roof tiles.

"The Eater of Dreams," he whispers in my inner ear. "Alas, our life is but a short night. The Baku will not have time to eat our dreams."

Jules goes shopping the third day, to buy farewell *omiyage* for her favourite students. I walk along the Philosopher's Path, from the Silver Temple, Ginkaku-ji, heading towards Kiyomizu Temple, criss-crossing the canals of Kyoto, wandering in a daze under the clouds of trees. Pale pink cherry blossoms lie scattered in the stone urns that are massed over with green moss, thick as wet velvet; cherry blossoms drift over the lion-faced stone dogs guarding the entrances to wooden houses; they float on the flat serene surface of the canals. I am falling under the spell of *sakura no hana.* They have no scent, they are as fragile as a dream. Lafcadio is silenced by their beauty.

The fourth day. Kiyomizu Temple. We climb upwards through narrow streets, lined with shops selling fans of silk, paper and ritual fans made of bamboo; Kyoto pottery and *kyo-yaki* ceramics; *cloisonné* jewelry and pillboxes; postcards, coasters, key chains, and pens; sake sets with two cups with no handles, a larger one for the male drinker, a matching smaller one for the female; long tubes of red and green fish kites for Children's Day; good luck charms for exams, their red, gold, and blue tassels dangling in bunches; Kyoto *washi*, delicate paper with gold and silver flecks pressed into a nubby, uneven surface; boxes and boxes of *omiyage* — bean-paste cakes and chocolate shaped like miniature temples and cherry trees. We wind our way up and up, along Chawan-zaka, Teapot Lane, towards the twin temples, finally reaching the bottom of the stairs framed by pines.

In the centre of the group of temples is Kyoto Jishu Shrine: the dwelling place of the god of love and matchmaking. In front of the shrine are two stones, several feet apart, both with ropes tied around them and jagged paper lightning bolts attached to the ropes. Groups of giggling school girls are lining up to walk from one stone to the other. Jules reads the notice aloud.

"If you can walk from one stone to the other with closed eyes, your love will be realized." She laughs and closes her eyes, staggering from one stone to the next in a parody of the uniformed girls, who laugh discreetly, hands over their mouths, at the *gai-jin* freaks making fools of themselves.

All around the temple are booths selling paper good-luck charms. I buy a paper inscribed with a love knot for a thousand yen, but I don't tie the paper to the board, where charms and wooden plaques, *ema*, testify to the efficacy of the god.

We leave the shrine, walking down the stairs, leaving behind the doubled temples, one larger, like the sake cup for males, the one beside it smaller, female, down out of the eastern hills of the city and come upon a Shinto graveyard. The grey markers of the dead blanket the hill in ascending terraces, like rice fields, but grey and black. Pillars incised with black kanji surround us. I think of graveyards at home: flat and neatly spaced, the rectangular graves and upright tombstones dotted with fluttering flags and fake-flower arrangements.

Even the dead crowd together here.

Laffy is with me, his ghost hovering around my head like a cloud of mosquitoes. "You have not performed the rituals for the one-year anniversary of Jeff's death. But here you can say good-bye."

"I think I'm going to rest here for a while," I say to Jules. "I've walked too much today. I'll catch a taxi back to the hostel later."

"Here?"

"Yes. It feels peaceful." I sit down on the square base of the nearest pillar. There are three small holes, an incense stand. Fallen cherry blossoms have left pink splotches against the stone.

"The flowers fade too swiftly," Laffy whispers. "Only in Japan did I understand the beauty of transience. Everything ends. Everyone dies. You understand that now, Elaine."

I touch the cold grey granite, trace the black kanji name. In my knapsack is the prayer. I will write my name and Jeff's above the love knot, take it home, leave it on his grave.

7. Reflections in Water

June 1 and the skies open. My new supervisor, Abe-sensei, tells me that rainy season lasts all month. Rain, rain, go away, I'll change my mind about staying in another day. It rains for two weeks, stops for one day, rains for two weeks more. *The Daily Yomiuri* calls it a "stagnant rainy season front." I feel stagnant. Wet clothes hang in my room, the futon feels flatter and harder every night, the musty tatami smells of damp straw. When it isn't raining, the humidity stays high, the temperature soars, and faster than Dorothy can throw a pail of water, I'm melting. I buy two tank tops and a short skirt at Daie, lie on my futon sweltering in the heat, watching *The Woman in the Dunes*. Monstrous women everywhere.

When I arrived back from Kyoto for the start of the new school year, Kawabata-sensei was gone, whirled away with no trace. My new supervisor is Abe-sensei, a compact man with a rare beard and a slight American accent. He's very excited when he hears I'm from San Francisco, telling me that he studied English for a year in San Diego. He used to teach in Hitachi. Suddenly I'm *sempai*, or as much of a *sempai* as a *gai-jin* can be. Abe-sensei asks my advice about the classes we teach together. He helps me fill out my forms for renewing, three months late. He invites me out for *okonomiyake*.

"You must try *okonomiyake*," he says. "It is very Japanese."

I don't tell him I've had it before. Instead, I smile, say *"Tanoshimi ni shite imasu,"* showing off my latest Japanese phrase. I'm learning deference, the soft-spoken way.

The local JET council organizes a joint Canada Day-Fourth of July party. The party is held in a second-storey bar off a side street, next to a flower shop with white buckets of roses, carnations, pink tulips, freesias, and clouds of baby's breath. Thirty of us gather on a muggy Saturday evening, spilling out of the small room, down the metal staircase, and into the street. I stand with Kim on the balcony, drinking white wine.

Kim looks unusually *soignée*, her hair up in a French twist, in loose linen trousers and a sleeveless fuchsia top. She's wearing sandals with a three-inch sole, but I still tower over her. I dropped twenty pounds when I was sick in March and I feel like a scarecrow, my clothes hanging off me.

Abe-sensei has implied that he'll turn a blind eye if I take August off without *nenkyu*, so I'm going back to the States. A stop in San Diego, and then to Abilene, to see my parents for the first time in four years. Click my heels three times. There's no place like home. There's no place like home.

Kim asks me, "So where are you going for your holidays?"

"San Diego and Kansas."

"Do you have friends in San Diego?"

Now is the time to tell someone about Jeff, someone besides Lafcadio. I wanted to tell Jules in Kyoto, but the words wouldn't come. I cannot keep this secret bottled up inside me forever.

"My fiancé's parents live there."

Kim smiles with interest. "I didn't know you're engaged. Why didn't he come over with you?"

"He died a year ago. He was biking home from work and a drunk driver hit him."

"Oh my God. I'm so sorry."

It's a conversation stopper, this death, a roadblock thrown between two people. I must learn to go around it.

I take out my wallet and show her Jeff's picture, a black and white shot from a photo booth. Jeff looks serious, frozen in a moment of stillness, his bald head and firmly set lips making him look like an adult. Usually, he looked about twenty. He was carded at most clubs. In the classroom he was hyper-kinetic, a whirling dervish. I sat in the still centre and he spun around me, shooting off light like a firecracker.

Kim glances at it. "Had you been together long?"

"Almost four years."

"That's a long time." After a pause, she says, "I broke up last month with my boyfriend, Mick. He's back home. We were supposed to live together next year, but I don't think that would work out. My Board of Education wouldn't approve."

She's not looking at me as she says this. There are layers beneath her words, but I don't need to know. We all carry our secrets, hidden beneath our skin.

All around me, I hear snippets of conversations. People exchanging addresses, making travel plans: Cambodia, Vietnam, Thailand, Bali, all the hot travel spots for the young and restless. I could attend the same farewell party in ten years and hear the same comments.

"Are you looking forward to going home," Kim asks.

How do I answer? Should I forgive my parents for not accepting Jeff? I don't know.

"I have to stay here for the orientation in Tokyo for the new teachers," Kim continues, ignoring my lack of response. "I thought I might do some travelling in Japan. Use a *ju-hachi kippu*, you know, the tickets that allow unlimited use on the local trains."

Her question turns into a reproach. I can leave, thanks to Abe-sensei. She's stuck here. August in Japan. I'm happy to escape.

Turning, I see my reflection in the large window of the bar, wavering against the glass. Kim's fuchsia top glows, the wine glass throwing off sparks of light.

Japan, a land of mirrors, endlessly reflecting back versions of itself. Lafcadio's Japan, the world of cherry blossoms and ghosts, Kyoto temples and geishas, may be one reflection, but I've seen something else. In my luggage are ten strands of origami cranes, each string hung with twenty *tsuru*. I couldn't reach that mystical number, one thousand cranes, my fingers not designed for the delicate work. The early cranes look like folded paper hats with uneven corners. I will drape the strands and the love knot I purchased in Kyoto over the stone on Jeff's grave, light incense, and say good-bye. Maybe then I will not be haunted.

Pressure on my temples from the approaching storm. Behind the crimson symbol of the Daie department store, shining like a red button, the sunset is a blurred orange smear. Cigarette smoke drifts up the stairs. The air smells of gasoline, hot tar, spilled beer, overlaid with a whiff of freesias and roses. The rain starts, a few sprinkles, then falls in thick, warm ropes. Shrieks and laughter from the people caught out on the street as the rain drums on the iron stairs.

I have other pictures of Jeff and me, taken in the same booth. We had to get photos for our JET applications; we took four serious shots and then one set of four together. In one we're mugging it up, making peace signs, sticking out our tongues, and squinting at the camera. The second is a blur; he was sitting down and I was turning so I could sit on his lap. A shot with both of us laughing, our faces side by side, black and white. We look like an overexposed negative, all contrast. In the fourth picture, we're kissing. All I can see is the back of his head, my fingers like white ribbons across his neck.

The day before I leave, Little Yasuko and two other girls from my English club stop by my desk. It's a school cleaning day, and they all look about twelve in their matching white and blue tracksuits, with their hair in pigtails. It's hard to believe they'll be graduating next March.

"I hope you have good visit with parents, Miss Elaine," Fumi says. I've told the students I'm going home for a holiday. Sometimes I wonder what pictures my students have in their minds of my home, what 1950s *Father Knows Best* version of America. Or maybe they see a prairie town, buildings with false fronts lining the street in a Clint Eastwood western.

Little Yasuko hands me a small pink and gold box made of paper.

I stand up to accept the gift politely and bow. "*Domo arigato gozaimasu.*" Taking off the lid, I see a pair of red paper earrings, small origami cranes, attached to gold studs. The English club girls have frequently admired my changing earrings: gold hoops, silver stars, green four-leaf clovers. A magical selection. At Christmas, I alternated tiny snowflakes with flashing Christmas tree lights.

Checking the staff room to make sure none of the other teachers are watching, Fumi lifts a braid and shows me her own pierced ears. She's wearing clear plastic studs to avoid detection.

"These are *tsuru,*" Yasuko instructs me. "Origami cranes. They will bring you luck."

"Thank you very much. They're lovely." I hold up an earring to admire it. Each wing is precisely folded. Nestled in my palm, the tiny bird looks as if it's about to take flight. "Would you like me to bring you some *omiyage* from California?"

The girls confer in Japanese, giggling, and then ask for posters of some boy band. I promise to buy each of them a poster and make a mental note to myself to buy a CD. Hopefully, the song lyrics aren't too obscure and will adapt to a teaching plan.

Little Yasuko lingers by my desk for a moment after the other two girls leave.

"I hope you will have a good trip, Elaine-san. You will be happy to see your parents."

I think for a moment. Perhaps I have learned forgiveness in Japan, the ability to move beyond my anger, at Jeff for dying, at my family for not accepting our relationship.

"When you see your family, you should say, *O-sashiburi desu ne.*"

"It has been a long time since I've seen them," I agree.

She smiles that teacher's smile. "Oh, very good."

At the airport, I thread through the crowds, amazed at the number of *gai-jin*. In my small village, I'm a rare species, the only blue-eyed blonde. Here, I'm part of the herd. On my way through security, I deposit the departure tax, two thousand yen, into a green vending machine.

The dead travel with me. I have the love knot for Jeff's grave. Lafcadio has been silent since I left Kyoto, since I began living my life in the present time, but sometimes I hear echoes of his voice. I bought one of his books, *Writings from Japan*, in a Tokyo bookstore; the archaic prose still weaves its magic.

The Eater of Dreams

The plane taxis down the runway. I look out the rain-splattered window and see the green trees, dripping water, the puddles on the tarmac reflecting the cloudy sky. The rain is easing off; it will be clear tonight. This is my favourite moment, the engines firing, the moment of anticipation as the plane leaves the ground.

NOTES AND ACKNOWLEDGMENTS

Earlier versions of several of the stories have been published in journals and anthologies. Thank you to all the editors.

"Spirit Houses" in *PRISM international*
"Whyte Noise" in *subTerrain*.
"White-Out" in *40 Below: Volume 2*
"Dancing the Requiem" in *Prairie Fire*
"Cutting Edge" in *Paperplates*
"Truth or Fiction." *The New Quarterly*
"The Heart is a Red Apple" in *NonBinary Review 6*
"Variations on a Theme" in *Lichen*
"*Gai-jin* Ghost" in *The New Quarterly*
"*Tasogare*" in *Prairie Fire*
"The Eater of Dreams" in *Descant*

"Dancing the Requiem" won first prize in *Prairie Fire's* Writing Contest 2018.

"The Apostles" won the Sir Charles G.D. Roberts Prize for Creative Fiction

"Zoonis County" is dedicated to Jeff.

The title and the poem (with translation) in "The Eater of Dreams" are from Lafcadio Hearn's *Kotto: Being Japanese Curios with Sundry Cobwebs*, 1904, copyright Project Gutenberg.

Information about Canmore history in "How You Look at Things" is from "Canmore Miners, Canmore, AB" on *The World of Lawrence Chrismas* website.

Quotations from Lafcadio Hearn are from Lafcadio Hearn's *In Ghostly Japan*. Boston, 1899, and *Writings from Japan: An Anthology*. Penguin, 1995.

Writing this book has been a long journey and I've been helped by many people along the way.

Thank you to all my friends in Japan. The JET crowd: Selena and Jim, Carmel, Komal, Adam, Greg, William and Annie, James, and Jane. To my students and colleagues at Chuo Secondary School and Mito Nikko, especially Miyake-sensei and Marcella. And to my friends in Omitama: Liz, Pumpkin Lady, Fumi, and especially Tomoyoshi and Harumi (my Japanese *obasan*).

To my cousins, thanks for the Zoonis County years and the memories.

Thank you to the professors at the University of New Brunswick for creating such a vibrant space for writers. "Searching for Spock" owes its current shape to Mark Jarman's suggestion of smashing two stories together. Thank you to all the fiction writers: Denis, Kelly, and Sean. And thanks to the PhD women — Robin, Lee Ellen, and Kathleen — for their fantastic camaraderie.

Thank you to Al and Jackie Forrie at Thistledown Press for believing in this book. I am so grateful to see these stories in print. Thank you to Harriet Richards for her impeccable editing skills.

Thanks to Kristy and Derrick, my first editors, who always suggested just the right word.

Finally, thank you to my parents, my sister Kristy, and my brothers Stuart and Jon, for always supporting my writing dreams. And love to my Derrick, for his honesty, his humour, and his hugs.

KAT CAMERON was born in Swift Current, Saskatchewan. She has an MA in Creative Writing from the University of New Brunswick and has worked for two years as an ESL teacher in Japan. Her debut collection of poetry, *Strange Labyrinth*, was published by Oolichan Books in 2015. Her fiction, poetry, and book reviews have appeared in over fifty journals and anthologies in Canada and the United States, including *The Antigonish Review*, *Canadian Literature*, *Descant*, *The Fiddlehead*, *Forage*, *Grain*, *Literary Review of Canada*, *NonBinary Review*, *Paperplates*, *Prairie Fire*, *PRISM international*, *The New Quarterly*, *Room*, *subTerrain*, *40 Below: Volume 2*, and *Beyond Forgetting: Celebrating 100 Years of Al Purdy*. Her poems have been shortlisted for the *Malahat Review*'s Far Horizons Award for Poetry and *FreeFall*'s Prose and Poetry contest. She teaches English literature and writing at Concordia University of Edmonton.